TRAPPED IN THE SLICKROCK CANYON

A MOUNTAIN WEST ADVENTURE

by

Gloria Skurzynski

Illustrated by Daniel San Souci

LOTHROP, LEE & SHEPARD BOOKS

NEW YORK

Library of Congress Cataloging in Publication Data

Skurzynski, Gloria.
    Trapped in the slickrock canyon.

    (A Mountain west adventure)
    Summary: Usually antagonistic, Gina and Justin, twelve-
year-old cousins, come to a better understanding of each other
during a night trying to survive a flash flood and other dangers
in the western mountains.
    [1. Cousins—Fiction. 2. West (U.S.)—Fiction] I. Title.
PZ7.S6287TR   1984   [Fic]   83-14988
ISBN 0-688-02688-5

Printed in the United States of America.

First Edition

9 10 11 12 13 14 15 16 17 18

For
DAVID SEAN NOLAN

I'm grateful for the valuable information about the canyonlands I received from range conservationist Jan Knight, archaeologist Marian Revitte, cartographer Ted Alm, all with the Bureau of Land Management, and ranger Ron Sutton of the National Park Service. And special thanks go to Stuart Ruckman, who taught me about rock climbing.

CONTENTS

1.

ON THE TRAIL

My cousin Justin's neck looked the same color as his hair. I noticed because he was walking ahead of me. Beneath the brim of his cowboy hat, it was hard to see where his short hair ended and the suntanned skin of his neck began.

Most of the boys in my school have cowboy hats, and some of the girls, too—I'm one of the girls who do. But they're hundred-dollar hats with fancy feathers around the band and genuine turquoise decorations.

My cousin Justin's was a plain old beat-up cowboy hat. And his boots were plain old beat-up cowboy boots. Justin *is* a cowboy, even though he's only twelve, the same age I am.

"Gina, if we're gonna git where we're goin' before the sun burns through your belly-hole,

you better move your feet in them fancy boots of yours."

That Justin! His grammar is perfect most of the time. Whenever I'm around, though, he puts on the country-Western accent as thick as the dust in Hickville. I live in the West too, but in the big city of Denver, people don't drawl through their noses. Or use words like "belly-hole."

Actually, the town where Justin goes to school is named Harkville, not Hickville. I call it Hickville just to make him mad, and it works. "Justin," I'll ask him, "how's the football team at Hickville Middle School this year?" and Justin will get this furious look on his face while his ears turn redder and redder. The truth is, all the kids who go to Justin's school are bused long distances from ranches, so they can't have after-school sports. *My* school has a maximal sports program.

Justin slowed down a little bit on the trail ahead of me. "Gina? Know what a cow puckie is?" he called back over his shoulder.

I sighed, hoping he could hear the sarcasm in my sigh. "I can just imagine what it is."

"Know what a cow puckie looks like?"

"Justin, don't be so gross."

"Waaal, ma'am," he drawled, "if you know what a cow puckie is, and you know what a cow puckie looks like, why'd you just step in one with them fancy boots?"

"*Eeeeeeee!*" I yelled, looking down at my brand-new hiking boots. They were perfectly clean. Not a speck of cow manure dirtied the soles or anywhere. I should have known—we'd been hiking at about seven thousand feet, and no cow in its right mind would have climbed that high.

"You're sickening!" I shouted. That made him laugh all the harder.

Everyone has heard of sibling rivalry, but I wonder if there's a word for rivalry between cousins. Whatever it is, Justin and I had plenty of it.

The trail was turning steep. It was covered with loose shale that made climbing slippery, especially for Justin in his smooth-soled cowboy boots. At least Justin's boots were broken in. My hiking boots were brand-new and felt stiff as steel. Even though I was wearing really good, thick ragg wool socks from L. L. Bean, I could feel the boots rubbing my heels.

If I'd been on that trail by myself, I wouldn't have had to hike so fast just to show Justin I could keep up with him. Alone, I could have sat down for a while to rest my heels and enjoy the scenery. The scenery really was maximal—not as spectacular as the Grand Canyon, a few hours' drive from there, but still awesome. Cliffs the colors of old and new pennies stood against a sky

so blue it looked like that hard-to-mix pottery glaze my mother can make so well. Far, far in the distance, white clouds piled high on top of each other like huge cotton balls. The sky behind those distant clouds was gray, though, not blue.

Two birds as big as pigeons, but not as fat, hopped around beneath a pine tree nearby, making funny screechy noises. The birds were gray and blue, too, like the faraway sky. Lots of gray and blue around, on that September morning. Almost the same as black and blue—the way I'd felt inside for so many months.

Actually, it wasn't the maximal scenery or a chance to bird-watch that made me want to slow down. It was my sore heels. Justin had me nearly running to keep up with him. I needed to sit down for a while if I was going to save my heels from a bad blistering. Right about then I saw my chance.

"Ow!" I yelled. "Wait, Justin. My hair's caught!"

My long hair really was caught, in the branches of a juniper tree. What Justin hadn't seen while he was charging ahead was that I'd twisted the hair, myself, around the feathery green twigs of the juniper.

Justin stopped. Maybe he needed a rest as much as I did. I took longer than necessary to unsnarl my hair from the tree. Then I pulled my mirror from one back pocket of my jeans and my brush from the other, and plunked myself down on a boulder.

"You're going to brush your hair?" Justin asked, his voice rising in a squawk. "Who cares what your hair looks like? There's hardly another person besides us in this whole part of Arizona, and I sure as heck don't give a good crud what your hair looks like!"

How gross he is, I thought while I went on brushing my hair and looking at myself in the hand mirror. The longer I could keep Justin standing there shooting off his mouth, the longer I could rest my heels.

"Hurry up, you dumb female," he finally yelled at me. "Don't you see those clouds over there in the southwest?"

I wasn't sure where southwest was, but I looked around at every bit of sky I could see. The only clouds were that high pile of fluffy ones I'd noticed before. Only now they weren't so white. They'd turned gray on the bottoms.

"You mean those clouds way over there?" I asked him, really puzzled, not just pretending. "They must be a hundred miles away. Aren't they?" We were up high enough that we could see for a hundred miles, and that's no exaggera-

tion. I didn't know why clouds so far away should worry Justin, when the sky over our heads was totally cloudless.

Justin clamped his lips down tight and looked at me as if he couldn't believe my ignorance. "Just move your butt," he growled, turning around and stomping off.

I stuck my tongue out at his back. He really was barf-making. He acted as if it had been *my* idea to go see a boring old petroglyph. I'd already seen a picture of a petroglyph in a schoolbook. I didn't need to hike halfway up the world just to look at some art an ancient Indian had chipped into rock.

Calling Justin certain poisonous names in my head, but not out loud, I got up and followed him. "Well, here go the old heels again," I muttered to myself so that he couldn't hear me. I'd never let on to Justin that I was hurting. Over the past few months, I'd become really good at hiding pain.

It was getting hot, about eighty degrees, and we didn't have any water with us because we hadn't planned this hike. Justin wasn't totally cruel, though. After a while he pointed out a little spring seeping out of the rock, almost hidden by some ferns. We both drank from cupped hands, letting the water dribble down our chins.

As we got close to the top of the mountain, the trail wasn't quite so steep. I'd been plodding along for what seemed like forever, trying to ignore my heels, when suddenly Justin stopped dead.

"What's the—" I started to ask, but he turned on me with a fierce look. His hand shot up in a 'keep quiet!' position. That's when I heard the noise, too: a faint, high whine like a dentist's drill.

"Stay here," Justin whispered to me. He walked away—or really, what he did was creep in the direction of the sound.

No way was Justin going to leave me alone up there in the wilderness. I tiptoed after him. The farther we went, the louder the noise became, so I don't know why we were bothering to sneak along that way. No one could have heard us over the noise anyway.

The sound was something like a saw in the woodworking class at my school, only harsher. More like ten thousand pieces of chalk screeching on a blackboard all at the same time. Then the sound grew so loud that I knew we had to be getting close to whatever was making it.

Justin had gone not quite to the edge of the cliff and was half-crouched, stretching himself forward inch by inch to peer down over the rim.

What kind of silly cowboy-and-Indian game was he playing, I wondered. I walked right up to him and asked, "Who do you think you are? Tonto?"

That's when my crazy cousin Justin grabbed me and knocked me down to the ground.

2.

AT THE SUMMIT

Why should I feel sorry for her? She has everything.

The day before that Labor Day weekend when Gina and her dad came to visit us, my mother clucked around the kitchen like an old hen. "Poor Gina," she said. "Poor little kid."

"Poor Gina!" I'd yelled. "What's poor about Gina? She owns her own purebred Arabian horse. Why, shoot, it costs more to stable that horse for one month than I make working on this ranch for a whole year."

"Now, now, Justie," my mom had fussed, "you ought to know by now that money isn't everything. And you know why I said 'poor little Gina.' How'd you like it if your mother just upped and took off like Gina's mother did? Throwing pots! *Hmpf!*"

Throwing pots. When I first heard it said, I thought Gina's mother had just gotten a mad spell on her and had thrown pots and pans around the kitchen to let off steam. That wasn't it at all. Seems Gina's mother, my Aunt Gwen, had been learning to make pots out of clay. That's what "throwing pots" means. You throw the clay onto a wheel that spins around, so you can shape a vase or a pot or something while the wheel's turning.

Aunt Gwen got pretty good at it. And then, for some reason, she decided she could throw pots better in San Francisco than in Denver. So she just headed off one day, leaving Gina and her father, my Uncle Dylan, all by themselves.

Maybe I should have felt sorrier for Gina after her mom left like that. But to tell the truth, Gina and I never could stand each other, not from the time we were tiny little kids. She always had to have the best—clothes, that Arabian horse, her rich private school in Denver. I worked for everything I got. I'd been working on my dad's ranch ever since I could walk. And figuring how hard I worked, I never did earn much spending cash. Hardly any.

My dad and Gina's father are twin brothers. Gina's father even got a fancier name—Dylan. After high school, Uncle Dylan left the ranch and learned to be a doctor, an orthopedic surgeon. He fixes people who break their bones skiing. Since there are lots of skiers in Denver, Uncle Dylan is pretty rich.

My dad's name is William—just plain Bill. He stayed on the family ranch here in northern Arizona. He works me hard, and he works himself a lot harder, but we just barely keep the ranch going.

That day—the day I took Gina to see the petroglyph—was the first day my dad had taken off from ranch work in a whole year. He took the time off so he and Uncle Dylan could go climb Muleskin Cliff, like they'd done once before when they were a lot younger. Uncle Dylan had brought special mountain-climbing gear from Denver: strong nylon rope, chocks, carabiners, and slings, stuff my dad could never have afforded to rent, let alone buy. Uncle Dylan does a lot of mountain climbing, so he has top-of-the-line equipment.

I really wanted to watch those two men climb. Gina and I were supposed to stay at the bottom while our fathers worked themselves up the sheer sandstone face of the cliff. I'm too young and inexperienced to climb a slickrock canyon wall. Still, I'd have given anything to try it.

"I'll need you to stay down there and cheer

me on, Jus," my dad had told me earlier. "My climbing skills have gotten kind of rusty lately."

I wasn't a bit worried about him. My dad's in great shape because he works outside in the open all the time. Uncle Dylan, I noticed, had the start of a pot belly beneath his belt.

At Muleskin Cliff, Uncle Dylan took the lead, finding handholds and footholds that were just little chicken-head knobs hardly wide enough to get a hold on. My dad was beneath him as they started up. A nylon rope stretched nearly straight down between them. Uncle Dylan wore Levi's and a bright yellow nylon windbreaker. My dad had on Levi's and an old blue sweater. Both of them were real easy to see against the reddish-orange face of Muleskin Cliff.

They'd reached about fifty feet above ground level when a foothold knob broke off beneath Uncle Dylan. My dad was belaying him—the rope was around Dad's waist so he could feed it out as Uncle Dylan fell. At the bottom of the drop, Uncle Dylan's weight made the rope slip through my dad's hands faster and farther than it should have. But he'd fallen no more than twelve feet before the line caught tight and held.

Well, you'd have thought her father was in deadly danger, the way Gina screamed when he fell. She started to cry and sob, "Daddy, Daddy! Come back down. You'll get killed! Uncle Bill's not a good enough climber! He doesn't know how to belay."

Not good enough? *My* father? Just because he'd let the rope slip a little! I felt like punching out Gina right then and there, except I don't punch girls, and she was already crying.

She stood there bawling like a calf, something about she couldn't stand it if anything happened to her father. So nothing would do but that my dad and Uncle Dylan had to come back down to ground level.

While Uncle Dylan talked to Gina to settle her down, my dad took me aside. "Listen, Jus, you're going to have to take her away from here," he told me, "far enough that she can't watch us climb. Why don't you guide her up the trail to see the old Indian petroglyph?"

"I want to watch you climb," I'd argued.

"Come on, now," my dad said, "have a little pity on your cousin. She's been through a lot lately, with her mother taking off like that."

My three older sisters say I'm spoiled, being the baby of the family and the only boy. They say I can talk our mom and dad into anything. But I can tell when I don't dare argue with my father, and that was one of those times. Seemed

like he *needed* to climb that risky slickrock wall with Uncle Dylan. At the time I thought it was because he had to prove he was as good a man as his rich, famous twin brother. Or that he was better.

By then, Uncle Dylan had quieted Gina. He and my dad stayed down on the ground, waiting until Gina and I got far enough away that we couldn't see them start the climb again.

Shoot, was I heck-fire mad! My ears felt like they were burning right off. "Waaal, Gina, ma'am, you've gummed up the whole dad-burned works just like always," I told her. I was using my old-time hick cowboy talk on her because she hated it. I learned to talk that way from seeing Chill Wills and Andy Devine in ancient cowboy movies on TV. I guess I talked like that around Gina because *her* talk was so high-and-mighty. *"Maximal,"* she always said. Everything was maximal. Why couldn't she just say "great" or "fantastic"? "Maximal" made her sound stuck-up and snotty.

She still had tears in her eyes, but did that make me feel sorry for her? Huh-uh! No, sir. Well, maybe I felt a little bit sorry, because I don't like to see anyone hurting. But even if I'd wanted to be nice to her, I didn't know what to say or how to begin. Gina never mentioned anything about her mother going away to San Francisco, so how could I?

I was mad, too, because she had on those dang hiking boots just made for steep trails like the one we were on. My boots—the ones I always wore, the only pair I owned—slipped all over the loose shale. Just to show that I could do better in my battered old cowboy boots than she could in her expensive new hiking ones, I set a pace up that trail that would have worn out a mountain lion.

Those boots made Gina into one heck of a good climber, though. She stuck right with me.

Only once did she stop, when her hair got caught on a juniper. That long, dark hair that curled halfway down her back—she should have twisted it into a pigtail or something so it wouldn't get caught anymore. Instead, she started to brush it.

Watching her, I got mad all over again. Even her shirt looked rich and snobbish! "Ski Vail," it said.

Ski Vail! Hah! Wouldn't I just like to ski Vail! All I can afford is to go tubing in the summer down a canyon stream, because that's free. My anger made me mean-mouth Gina, though I know I shouldn't have.

To hurry her so we could move along, I men-

tioned those thunderheads over the Grand Wash
Cliffs, eighty miles to the southwest.

"But those clouds are so far away," she said.
"Why worry about clouds way over there?"

Shoot, I thought, if she was too dumb to know
about rain in the canyonlands, she'd probably be
too dumb to appreciate my petroglyph when she
saw it.

I don't know which white man first laid eyes
on that petroglyph, but it might have been me.
The October I was eight, I'd gone with my dad
on the deer hunt. That year I was still too young
to actually hunt, so I'd hung around the campfire
in the morning by myself, until the sun got high
enough that I didn't need the fire's heat to keep
warm.

After that, I followed some bighorn sheep
tracks that led right off the rim of a cliff into
space. As I hunkered down to look over the rim,
I saw a ledge about ten feet beneath me. That
must have been what the wild mountain sheep
landed on. The ledge was easy to get to—I just
climbed down a rock outcropping.

When I reached the ledge, there was this bighorn sheep. Not a live one like the one I'd been
tracking, but a sheep carved into the desert varnish that coated the red rock. The sheep's horns
curved way back over its head in two parallel

lines that looked like an art design, but other than that, it seemed quite true to life. And beside the sheep was the flute player.

He must have been playing music to that sheep for a thousand years. The flute player had been chipped into the rock by the ancient ones, the Anasazi, the Indians who lived there long before white men came. As the wind on the ledge blew around my ears, I stared at the flute player and seemed to hear the music of the Anasazi. Sort of sad, sort of mysterious, a song that went straight through into my feelings. I couldn't wait to share the magic with my dad.

Now my dad was making me show my petroglyph to Gina, someone I didn't even like. What right did she have coming to my part of the world, anyway? Why couldn't she have stayed in the big city with her snobby friends?

I tramped ahead of her, mad as could be. We hadn't gone too far past Maidenhair Springs— that's my own name for it, because of the ferns —when I heard a funny noise. Something like a whole hive of honeybees buzzing, only far away. Right off I knew it wasn't natural. There's nothing on those mesas that can make a sound like that.

The closer we came to topping off the ridge, the better I could tell that the sound was some

kind of machinery noise, coming from right around my petroglyph. And I had a suspicion about what was making that noise, a terrible suspicion that made me angry and worried. Worried enough that I wasn't about to march up to the rim, where I'd be right overhead of whoever was on that ledge. At least not till I sneaked a look first, to find out what they were doing.

Cautious as a kit fox, I poked my head forward to see. And then there came old Gina, big as a tuba and twice as brassy, showing herself like a target against the bright blue sky above the ridge.

Sometimes you just can't take the time to argue with a person. If I'd said, "Gina, I don't know who's down there, but it's likely to be mean, dangerous men up to no good, and bad men can hurt people"—if I'd said that, I guarantee you Gina would have mouthed off with a dozen different questions and arguments. So to save time, I just knocked her away from the rim. With a few quick, whispered words, spoken while I was sitting on her, I convinced her to keep her mouth shut.

Gina wasn't hurt at all from the knocking over I gave her. I'd pushed her kind of gentle, not like I'd tackle a guy. What surprised me, even her feelings weren't hurt for a change. Her eyes got wide with curiosity, though I could tell she didn't believe me about the danger. Belly down, we both crawled in the red dust toward the edge so we could have a look.

What we saw was what I'd thought likely. Two men with a gasoline-powered rock saw were trying to cut my petroglyph out of the cliffside. Those rotten scuds! No one's allowed to take Indian artifacts away from where they're found. It's against the law!

There was nothing I could do to stop them. Nothing I dared do, because on the ground next to them lay a high-powered rifle. Beside it were a crowbar and a grease can.

The men were taking turns using the rock saw, which looked heavy, and which was grinding rock and spitting oil something wild. Both men were spattered with oil and powdered with red sandstone. The taller one had on a faded plaid shirt and a roped-up bandana tied around his forehead as a sweatband. The other had a beard and wore a dirty undershirt that showed his tattooed shoulders. They were so busy with the hard, noisy work that they didn't notice Gina and me. Thank heaven for that, because our heads were no more than five feet above theirs.

That was too close for comfort. I pulled Gina's arm to signal her to snake backward. When we

were far enough from the rim, we ran in a crouch to a place about forty feet farther down the ridge, where we could hide behind a big boulder. That way we could keep an eye on those two guys, but they weren't likely to see us.

"What are they doing?" Gina asked me after we were hidden.

"They're vandals. They're stealing the petroglyph I was going to show you."

"Why would they want to do a thing like that?" she asked.

"Because it's worth a lot of money, dummy. Plenty of people would pay lots of bucks for an ancient Indian rock carving to hang on their wall."

From where we were I had a good view of the steep side of the mesa, from right beneath us all the way down to the valley floor. Something caught my eye and made me catch my breath. On the side of the mesa, climbing almost hand over hand because of the steepness, came a third man.

That country is usually so empty that you never see a soul in it for a whole week. All of a sudden, the place was practically crawling with people, like downtown Flagstaff. At first I thought the man was another one of the petroglyph vandals. But as he climbed, he stopped

every now and then to hold something dark against his face, as if he was aiming it at the rock thieves. Didn't look like a pistol he was holding, though, and it didn't fire.

Down at the bottom of the mountain, in a gully, I saw two outfits parked—a pickup truck and a jeep. The jeep was tan, with a green-and-blue circle on the side. The Bureau of Land Management symbol.

Those two creepy-looking guys cutting the petroglyph could in no way have been connected with the Bureau of Land Management, a government agency that *protects* the wilderness. So that had to mean that the man hauling himself up the rock wall was the driver of the BLM jeep. As he got closer, I could see that it wasn't a gun he held up to his face, but a camera.

Gina and I had taken the long, curving trail up the slope to the mesa top, and it wasn't all that easy. The BLM man was crawling right up the steep, rocky side of the mesa, which was a lot shorter in distance but about a hundred times harder. It was several minutes after I saw him that Gina noticed him. She poked me and raised her eyebrows in a question.

"Bureau of Land Management," I whispered. "Looks like he's taking pictures of those guys, to use as evidence."

"How did he happen to be here right now?" she asked.

"How should I know?"

"He'd better be careful," Gina whispered. "They might shoot him. From where he is, he can't see the gun they have on the ground. Maybe we ought to warn him."

"If we warn him, they'll shoot *us!*" I whispered in her ear.

"I thought you were supposed to be a big, brave cowboy," she muttered, looking disgusted with me. Before I could stop her, she picked up some pebbles and tossed them down the mountain, to get the BLM man's attention. She hadn't thrown them far enough, so she scooped up another handful.

"Stop that!" I hissed at her. "Don't make him look at us. He's got to keep his eyes on the two crooks so he can watch their moves. If they turn around and start shooting, he needs time to duck."

Gina bit her lip, and for once didn't answer back.

It was the worst, scariest feeling to watch that BLM man climb closer to my petroglyph. I keep calling it my petroglyph, as though it belonged to me, but the government land it was on really belongs to every U.S. citizen. And a government

man was climbing up to try to save the petro-glyph. I wished I could help him, or warn him some way, but I didn't know how to do either.

The two vandals had their hands full as the rock saw cut deeper and deeper into the red sandstone. The one with the bandana headband had taken his turn operating the saw; the other was holding on to the corners of the slab they were cutting to keep it from falling down when it broke loose. If it fell, it could smash to worth-less pieces.

It kept them busy enough that they still didn't notice Gina or me. They didn't notice the BLM man, either, and they couldn't hear him coming because of the noise from the saw. As we watched, he stopped not twenty feet below them to take more pictures. He was so close that I could see the sweat on his face from his hard climb.

Just then the power saw jammed or something —it sputtered to a stop. The guy with the head-band swore some really raunchy words I bet Gina had never heard before. When he leaned over to pick up the grease can, he caught sight of the BLM man. He dropped the grease can fast and grabbed for the rifle.

"Well, lookie here," he said, aiming the rifle at the BLM man. "We got a tourist taking our pic-tures, seems like."

The vandal in the undershirt kept holding the sandstone—it was so close to being sliced all the way through that if he let go, it would shear off and break—but he twisted around to see what was happening. "Who is he, Jaggers?" he asked.

"Why don't you just come on up here, man, so we can find out who you are?" Jaggers said, wiggling his fingers around the trigger.

The BLM man scrambled up to the ledge. His face was pale beneath the sweat, but he clutched the camera that hung from a strap around his neck as though he intended to protect it.

"Who is he, Jaggers?" the tattoo guy asked again.

"I'm an archaeologist with the Bureau of Land Management. I was checking a site in that side-canyon down there when I heard your saw," the man said. "You're removing an antiquity. That's a felony punishable by a ten-thousand-dollar fine and a year in prison."

"So who's gonna arrest us, huh?" Jaggers said. Grinning mean-like, he reached out to take the camera, but the BLM man backed away.

"Gimme that sucker," Jaggers hollered, lunging forward.

The BLM man ducked sideways, then jerked the strap off his neck and flung the camera way out—it made an arc in space before it fell into the gully. I guess he figured the film might some-

how be saved, even if the camera got smashed.

"So you want to play games, huh?" Jaggers snarled, poking the man in the chest with the rifle barrel. "You want games, I'll give you games." Another poke in the chest.

The jabs had knocked the BLM man off balance. When he reached toward the rock face to keep himself from falling, Jaggers gave him one more shove, this time a lot harder, with the rifle butt.

Arms flung sideways, shirttail flapping in the wind, the BLM man pitched backward off the ledge, his spread-eagled body outlined for a split second against the sky as he dropped. My stomach lurched. The chasm he fell into was two hundred feet straight down.

Gina screamed, and screamed, and kept on screaming.

3.

UNDER ATTACK

It had to be a nightmare. Pretty soon I'd wake up in my bed in Denver. Mother would hug me and say, "Don't cry, baby. It's only a bad dream."

Instead, it was Justin who was shaking me and yelling, "Gina, stop screaming! Get up! *Move!*"

He yanked me to my feet and pulled me to the shale-covered trail we'd climbed earlier. That's when the first bullet hit, puffing up the dirt near my feet. I'd never heard the noise of a real gunshot before, but right away I knew what it was. My dreamy, unreal feeling ended the second I heard that shot! I leaped forward as if I'd been jabbed with a meat fork, and ran down the trail faster than I'd ever run in my whole life. The pain in my heels? Funny how you forget pain when someone's shooting at you. You forget everything except to *run*!

"Is he coming after us?" I yelled at Justin, who was ahead of me, slipping and sliding in his worn boots.

"I don't know," Justin yelled back. Just at that instant another bullet pinged off a rock right over Justin's head.

"Cripe!" he yelped. "Keep low, Gina. Make yourself a small target. Don't look back!"

Until he said that, I hadn't even thought about looking back. Suddenly, the skin on the back of my neck started to feel creepy, as though dozens of tiny spiders were crawling over me. I wanted —needed!—to turn around and find out where Jaggers was. Or whether Jaggers was even the man chasing us; it might have been the other man, the one with the tattoo. Somehow, though, I knew it was Jaggers. He'd been holding the gun, and he looked mean enough to shoot at kids.

"Run fast!" Justin shouted. "Trail's starting to twist. Get to the twisty part—he won't be able to see us to shoot."

Even though we were on the top part of the mountain trail, where the slope was more gentle, I kept feeling I was on the verge of falling. Always off balance. Justin had an even harder time of it than I did, because of his boots.

Just then his feet sprawled out from under

him. As he fell to his hands and knees, his hat flew off. Running as fast as I was, I had to swerve to miss both the hat and Justin. While I swerved, I grabbed the back of Justin's shirt and jerked him to his feet.

What a maneuver! For a second or two, in spite of being terrified, I felt myself filling up with wild pride because I'd made such a great move. Like Wonder Woman. I got a surge going that carried me right past Justin.

"Thanks," he gasped, on his feet and running again, now behind me.

"Your hat . . ."

"Forget it," he yelled. "Not worth . . . getting shot for."

If we'd hiked fast on the way up that trail, it was nothing compared to the speed we made going down it. We passed the little spring where we'd stopped to drink, passed it a whole lot faster than I would have expected. Run, keep running! It's a good thing I was in maximal shape from being on the track team at school. But running downhill on that pebbly trail was a whole lot harder than on the dirt track at school. And compared to racing in Adidas, running in hiking boots was like having both feet in gallon cans of cement. Each foot seemed to weigh about fifty pounds. Still, I'd never before had so much in-

centive to win. My adrenaline must have been pumping like a spigot, because I sailed down that upper slope with breath to spare.

At first, that is. Then the trail got steep. The sense of speed started to wear away. Rounding each bend, we had to slow way down to keep from losing our balance. Sometimes we did fall sideways, but always managed to jump up fast.

Jaggers must have fallen too. From behind us, we heard a crash and then a rattling, tearing noise, as though he'd fallen and slid. After that we heard some really awful swearing. Jaggers' big fall bought us a little time, but all too soon his footsteps started again.

Running downhill is awful. The pain in my heels wasn't bothering me—now it was my toes that hurt. Because of the steepness, with each step my toes slid forward, getting mashed and battered against the stiff fronts of my hiking boots. My knees and hips began to ache—they were taking such a pounding from going down-hill—but the worst soreness of all was in my thighs. I was all worn out, with no second wind coming. It gave me that terrible feeling you sometimes have in a dream, when you try to escape from something horrible, but you can't move fast enough to get away. Only this was reality. Someone really was chasing me.

Or was he? Was Jaggers still behind us? Or had his thigh muscles begun to tighten and cramp the way mine had? Did he have a bad stitch in his side, like mine? Maybe he wanted to throw himself on the ground to rest for a minute. Only for a minute.

How much longer would I have to run before I reached my father? *Daddy, where are you?* A sob built up in my chest. Had to push it down.

"Are we far from bottom?" I called out to Justin.

"Not too far."

"Think he's still . . . chasing us?" No more shots had zinged around us since the second one.

"Stop a minute," Justin panted, grabbing my arm from behind. Both of us had been running so hard it took us half a dozen steps to come to a halt. Justin held his breath so he could hear better, and I did too. We heard him—Jaggers' footsteps pounded the trail somewhere behind us.

"Go!" Justin yelled, and we took off again, with Justin in the lead.

I was running all wrong: in a crouch, because of going downhill; taking short strides, because of the hiking boots; arms bent forward and sideways to keep balance; using my thighs as shock absorbers. Energy getting sapped fast. Seemed I'd been running for hours, though probably not

more than ten minutes. Longest race I'd ever run before . . . was 800 meters. On a regulation track. That mountain trail was longer than a mile, and it was wrong for running. All wrong.

Breath tore out of my lungs in fast, burning heaves. Stitch in side tortured me. "Have to stop!" I yelled at Justin, flinging my arms against the rock wall beside the trail to hold myself up.

Justin was in as bad a shape as I was. He dropped to his knees, sucking air, too winded to talk. Finally he got enough breath to point downhill and gasp, "Nearly bottom." Then, a couple of seconds later, "Listen! No steps!"

It was true. The man who was chasing us must have been as exhausted as we were. Had he stopped chasing us for good? Or was he just taking a rest?

Slowly, our breathing got easier. We'd started to pour sweat; my T-shirt was soaked, every thread of it. Justin and I sat with our legs stretched out, backs against the rock. And then, from behind us—how far behind we couldn't tell —came the crunch of footsteps on shale.

We looked at each other with doom on our faces. Pulling ourselves up, we started down the trail again. "Got to move," Justin mumbled, "or that big old mean guy's gonna nail us." Neither of us could move that fast. But the footsteps we'd heard hadn't been going so fast either.

At last, the bottom. On level ground, I started to get some breath back. Justin was ahead of me, but he was . . .

"Wait a minute, Justin," I yelled. "You're going the wrong way!"

"Come on," was all he answered, without turning around.

"Justin, this isn't the way we came."

He just kept going.

"Justin, stop! I want to go to my father. This isn't . . . the way to my father!" Between pants, my voice got higher and louder.

"Gina, you scud!" he exploded at me. "Can't you just come?"

"Not when you're going the wrong way!"

He grabbed my hand and tried to pull me, but I fought back. "I want my father," I shouted, nearly crying.

"If you don't move, I'm gonna hurt your little face," Justin hollered at me. His ears were burning red. "We can't go to our fathers. Think how they are—so easy to see against the cliff. Helpless! He'll shoot them like clay pigeons."

Into my mind came the picture of my father in his yellow windbreaker against the red cliff. Hanging on, hundreds of feet up, he could never protect himself from the man with the gun. Jag-

gers was trying to shoot Justin and me—if we ran straight to our fathers, Jaggers might shoot them, too. They'd be perfect targets on that red rock face.

The thought of his shooting my father terrified me. I was already so scared that it's hard to believe I could get a whole lot more frightened, but I did. I felt as though electric ice water poured through every part of my body, clear down to my fingernails.

I stopped fighting and ran after Justin. I'd wasted at least a minute arguing. Was Jaggers catching up to us because of me?

The argument had started because Justin made a turn down a side canyon. It was a narrow canyon with high, red rock sides showing only a patch of sky above. Sort of like being at the bottom of an elevator shaft with no roof, only the shaft went on and on.

The bottom of the canyon was full of pebbles, even more than on the mountain trail. But on the level surface, they weren't as slippery. There were other obstacles, though—big boulders on the ground. As the canyon got narrower and narrower, the boulders began to block our path. We had to climb over them, and my thighs just didn't want to climb. Also, my sweat-soaked jeans were chafing the skin behind my knees. I hurt in so many places I couldn't count them. My original pain—in my heels—was now just one more hurt in a long list of sore parts.

Justin climbed over a pile of boulders that totally blocked the narrow canyon bottom. Instead of going down the other side of the pile, he jumped to a ledge on one wall of the canyon and crept along it, his back to the wall, arms stretched sideways. "Follow me," he ordered.

I didn't have the energy to follow him onto that ledge; anyway, it looked too narrow. He wasn't watching me, so I just clambered down the far side of the boulder pile. The ground at the bottom looked sort of mucky, but with everything else that was happening to me, I wasn't worried about getting my feet wet.

I jumped down from the bottom boulder, but the ground didn't catch me. Instead, it reached up to suck me down. I felt as though I'd landed in thick Cream of Wheat. My feet sank into it . . . up over my ankles, creeping toward my knees, and still I kept on sinking.

"Justin!" I screamed.

"Oh my Lord!" he yelled. "You got into the quicksand!"

Quicksand! My heart stopped, then began to race like a clock gone mad. I yanked one foot, but it wouldn't come loose, and the other foot

sank even deeper. Frantic, I kept trying to pull out first one foot and then the other, but the harder I tried, the more I was swallowed by that oozy muck. Slowly it reached up and smothered my knees.

Justin was still on the ledge, searching for a way to come down to the canyon floor. "Don't struggle," he said. "You're not in any danger."

He must have realized how ridiculous that sounded—a man with a gun was chasing us, I was stuck fast up to my knees in quicksand, and Justin said I wasn't in any danger. Because he laughed then, a high, crazy giggle. "I mean, you're not in any danger from the quicksand," he explained. "Try moving your feet real slow. I'll come help you."

I tried so hard to do what Justin told me. Move slowly. I could push forward a little bit, but I was still too stuck to get out of the glue myself. Trapped! Helpless! And behind me came the steady crunch, crunch of Jaggers' boots. I was too terrified to even scream.

"Here." Justin had reached me, but didn't come all the way up to me. He was more than an arm's reach in front, standing in muck, too, swaying gently from side to side. But he stayed on the surface of the quicksand. It rocked like Jell-O beneath him.

"Grab this," he said. He'd picked up a broken branch and was holding it toward me. When I grabbed for it, I only caught some little dry twigs on the end; they broke off in my hand. Not till the third try did I get a good solid hold.

"Easy. Easy," Justin said, pulling the branch as he moved his feet backward, doing a bouncy, side-to-side dance. "Lift your feet out real easy. They'll come. Don't be scared."

Scared! I was way beyond scared. Past petrified. I'd reached a place where the fear was so big it didn't have a name. Jaggers' feet kept coming, coming, closer and closer. Justin and I were still hidden by the pile of boulders we'd crossed, but judging from the loudness of Jaggers' steps, we wouldn't be hidden long.

There's nothing more menacing than to be chased by someone you can't see, someone you can only hear. I knew it was a man behind me. I'd seen him on the mountaintop. But in my imagination he grew and grew until he became as big as a giant. If I'd been Justin, I might have turned around and run and left me stranded there. Justin's face looked so pale beneath his suntan. His eyes showed white all around the blue irises. But he kept steadily pulling that branch. To save me. Even after I'd treated him so mean.

At last one of my feet started to break loose, then the other, making loud sucking sounds and leaving holes in the muck. Holes that filled with ooze again as soon as my feet left them.

"That's the way, Gina. Move fast. Skate over it," Justin told me.

Soon . . . thank you, God . . . and you, Justie . . . I was on solid ground. But the pounding of boot heels on shale had gotten so loud that Jaggers couldn't have been more than thirty feet behind us.

"Come on," Justin said, grabbing my hand. I don't know where the energy came from, but both of us found the power to run. The pile of boulders and the twisting of the narrow canyon kept us from seeing Jaggers, and kept him from seeing us. I thought.

A deafening explosion crashed all around us—another gunshot. Jaggers must have spotted us. In the high, high walls of that slickrock canyon, walls getting so close together that in places we could almost stretch out our arms to touch both sides, the sound of that rifle blast bounced back and forth to echo like a cannon.

"Holy cripe! He could s-start a rockslide!" Justin stuttered, looking up as if he expected the red cliffs above us to crash down onto our heads. "And, oh my heck! Look at the sky! It looks like rain!"

I glanced up at as much sky as I could see between the towering cliffs. It was gray and cloudy.

"Rain. So big deal," I mumbled. If Justin hadn't been so nice to me such a short time before, I might have answered something smart-mouthy. I couldn't figure out why he kept yammering about clouds. It seemed to me we had a whole lot worse things to worry about than a chance of rain.

We went around a few more twists and bends, slowing down when we couldn't run anymore, sometimes lying flat on our stomachs to drag ourselves across rockpiles. Every few minutes we stopped to listen for Jaggers. He was always behind us—his footsteps, amplified like drumbeats, echoing between the canyon walls.

The last time we stopped, Justin listened harder than usual. His face twisted into a frown of concentration that suddenly turned to panic.

"Do you hear it?" he asked me, his voice squealing.

"Hear Jaggers? Yes, but he's no closer—"

"Not Jaggers. The other sound!"

Then, faintly, I did hear it. It sounded like . . . the only way I can describe it is like a train in a faraway tunnel.

"Up!" Justin almost screamed. "We've got to get up!"

"What's wrong?" I shrieked too, because his panic was contagious.

"Flood! It's a flood!"

"A flood? How can there be a flood when it isn't even raining?"

"Shut up!" Justin yelled. "We've got to get out of here! Got to get on high ground!"

Even while we spoke those few words, the roar became louder.

4.

ABOVE THE FURY

I lost my head.

For half a minute or so I ran around, yelling at the top of my lungs, from pure fear. I could hear that flood coming. Its powerful sound was roaring off the walls of a canyon not too far ahead of us.

Not that we didn't have a chance to outrace it. We might, if we turned right then and ran like crazy. The head of a flash flood isn't all that swift. I'd seen a couple of them before. The front edge of the water is shallow, and it sort of explores all the little bumps and holes on the ground before the flood builds to full force.

But if Gina and I turned and ran from the flood heading toward us, we'd have to run right into the sights of Jaggers' gun. Some choice! We could

choose to most likely die from drowning, or to for sure die from a bullet in the brain.

"Justin, what is it?" Gina yelled.

I couldn't answer her. Fear had put a clamp on my voice. Our only way out was straight up, which was impossible. They don't call those canyons "slickrock" for nothing. That's just what they are—smooth, straight up, and slick.

Without special climbing equipment, we could no more scale those slickrock walls than we could shinny up a skyscraper. So Gina and I were doomed. If we didn't drown in the flash flood, we'd get battered into dogmeat by the debris swept along in the rushing water.

"Justin, what's wrong?" Gina yelled again, finally getting through to me. Poor kid, she didn't understand. For all her smart mouth, she was just a dumb city kid, not used to Mother Nature going wild in the canyonlands.

By then I didn't have to answer her; I just pointed. From around a bend, mud-colored fingers of floodwater sneaked toward us, pushing dead leaves, pebbles, pine cones, and one very drowned lizard along the front edge.

The water had a strong earth smell to it, like a fresh plowed field in the springtime. I stood half hypnotized, watching the red stream puddle around my ankles. When it got to swirling around my boot tops—and that took no more than twenty seconds—I shook myself loose from the numbness and yelled, "Danged if I'm gonna stand down here and drown! Come on, Gina. Help me look for cracks in the rocks to use for handholds."

It couldn't have been more than fifteen seconds before Gina answered, "I can't see any cracks, but there are some holes."

"Holes! What holes! Where?" I sloshed over to the place she pointed at, and sure enough, there were holes in the rock. Holes about twelve inches apart, going straight up the rock in a line.

I gave a short, insane laugh because I hadn't been the one to discover the holes in the rock. It took Gina, the dumb kid from the city, to find them.

They were Moki steps, carved by the ancient Indians for climbing to an overhead storage ledge. From where I stood, I couldn't see the ledge, but it had to be there—Moki steps always lead to something.

"Quick, get over here," I hollered, grabbing Gina's hand to pull her because the water was getting deeper every second. Swifter, too. Broken tree branches and good-sized rocks got kicked up to the surface by the fast current, then plopped down and disappeared into the murky water.

The water—up to our thighs now—splashed

against Gina as I lifted her so she could set her foot in the bottom Moki step. "That's it, like climbing a ladder," I told her. "Or a telephone pole. Move your hands and feet up, one after the other. Get going!"

Why did it seem to take her so long, as if everything she did was in slow motion? I couldn't start my own climb until she'd gone past the bottom four holes. Water sloshed up to my waist—it was deepening that fast—and the current shoved hard against my legs. In another minute the flood would reach my armpits, then my nose. . . . The roar was already battering my eardrums. Seemed like every raindrop that had fallen into those faraway canyons that morning, plus every grain of dirt and grit and debris from the mountains, was rushing down on me all at the same time.

Just then a dead coyote floated past me, looking flattened because its coat was so soggy. *"For crud's sake, Gina, move yourself!"* I bawled, reaching up to give her butt-end a boost.

"I'm going! I'm going!" she shouted back. Finally I was able to get my own foot in the bottom Moki step and my hands in the holes above it.

If only I'd been a few seconds quicker! But I wasn't quick enough. A big log shot out of the current like a torpedo—it must have flipped off some obstruction underwater—and slammed my right foot against the canyon wall. I guess I screamed.

"*Now* what's wrong?" Gina wanted to know.

I couldn't answer. Pain filled my head in red and black waves. I managed to moan, "I think my foot got broken."

"Oh, no! Really broken? Can you put any weight on it?"

Clamping my back teeth together so I wouldn't cry out, I guided my hurt foot into the next Moki step. When I tried to haul myself up, I screamed again. Shocks of pain made me so dizzy I was afraid I'd fall into the flood. It wouldn't have been too far to fall—water slapped at the knee of the leg I had in the bottom Moki hole.

One thing I'll say for Gina—she sure is fast to understand a situation. Right away she pulled off her wide Western belt. From up above me, she leaned over and dangled the belt buckle in front of my eyes.

"Here," she said, "take this and slip it through your belt in front. Then loop my belt through its own buckle, and give me the end."

I guess I'm kind of swift, too, because right away I caught on to what she meant. It wasn't easy to do what she told me, though. My left

hand was hanging on to a Moki hole, my left foot was submerged, my right foot was useless. All I had to work with was one hand, and the leather of Gina's belt was thick and stiff.

Finally I got Gina's belt attached to my belt. When she leaned down again, I pushed the tip up to her.

"Okay, now we'll go one-two-three," she said. "On three you hop up with your good foot while I pull you."

It worked! With my hands in an overhead hole, I could jerk myself upward when Gina yanked me by the belt at the count of three. First Gina would climb a step, then she'd pull me up a step. My good foot kind of scrabbled from hole to hole.

It was slow going. What surprised me—after a while, my right foot stopped hurting. I guess it had gone into shock or something, because as long as I didn't bang it, or try to put any weight on it, it didn't bother me too much.

We were halfway up the Moki steps, maybe twenty feet above the flood, when the rain hit us. A real gully-whacker. It doesn't rain in the canyonlands very often, but when it does, it's likely to pound your head right down through your shoulder blades.

There we were, trying to crawl up a vertical

wall, with a flash flood crashing around underneath us, and the sky dumping tons more of water down on our heads. It would have made a good, scary horror movie. The only thing missing was alligators snapping at our ankles.

I realized then that one other thing was missing. Jaggers. If he hadn't managed to climb up off the ground, he'd already been swept away by that flood. Because by that time, *nobody* could stay alive in it, I guarantee you.

Fed by the cloudburst, that noisy, roaring flood went wild beneath us. It looked like a pot of butterscotch pudding at full boil, only redder. Boulders the size of bushel baskets bounced around like baseballs, with a weird, hollow, clonking sound. Torn-up trees got whipped along like little twigs, then split into toothpicks with cracking explosions. Just the *noise* was enough to scare a person spitless.

After a while Gina made it up to the ledge, pulling me after her. As we sat there panting, streaming water, I took a look around.

It was an open space nature had scooped out of the rock. The Anasazi must have used it for storage, the way I'd guessed. A broken wall made from stone and adobe showed where they'd built a bin, to keep their extra corn safe from animals like ground squirrels and chipmunks. Inside the wall sat a pot they'd probably used for scooping grain.

"Take your boot off," Gina said.

"Huh?"

"Do what I said. Right away." Her voice may have been shaky from fright, but the command was loud and clear.

"Who do you think you are, bossing me around?" I asked her. "Anyway, why should I take my boot off?"

"Because, if your foot's hurt that badly, it's going to swell. Maybe it's swollen already. Unless you get that boot off fast, the swelling's going to hurt so much you'll think that first pain was just a tickle."

"How do you know so much about it, smart-face?"

"My father's an orthopedic surgeon, remember?" She sounded like her usual stuck-up self. "Here, let me give that boot a pull."

Rain pounded, the flood roared, and thunder nearly busted the sky wide open, but my scream was louder than all of them put together.

"Hurts that bad, huh? I guess we're too late," Gina said, not the least bit worried that she'd dang near killed me with pain. "We'll have to cut off your boot."

After the agony died down enough that I

could talk, I asked her, "With what? Did you bring along your orthopedic scissors?"

That shut her up for a minute or two. She looked around the ledge. Nothing was there except the crumpled wall and that one pot. No arrowheads. No cutting tools.

Then her face lit up with that smart-eyed look, and she pulled her mirror from her jeans pocket. "With this!" she announced. Hitting it with a little rock, she broke the mirror into a couple of pieces.

I had to hold my ankle with both hands to keep it steady while Gina sawed at the side of my boot—good thing the leather was soft. Even so, it took her a long time; that broken glass wasn't anywhere near as sharp as a knife. Finally she managed to ruin my boot and get my mangled foot out.

"You can leave your sock on," she said. "That's a tube sock, so it will stretch if your flesh swells around the bandages."

"What bandages?" I asked.

Before I knew what she was up to, she'd whipped off her T-shirt.

My heck! I mean . . . Gina's my first cousin. Maybe we're related even closer than most first cousins, because our fathers are identical twins. But still! She just took off that old shirt like I wasn't even a male person, or like I was blind or something. I turned my head away as fast as I could, and clamped my eyelids shut for good measure.

With my head turned away, I didn't see what she was doing, but I heard cloth ripping. After the ripping stopped, Gina said, "You can look now. I won't contaminate your virgin eyes."

I felt the heat creep up into my cheeks. That Gina—she sure could make me feel like a baby. Cautious, I sneaked a look. Gina had her shirt back on, only now it was short, like a quarter-back's jersey.

When she reached toward me I jerked back, but she was only stretching my sock cuff to look at my ankle. I didn't want to look.

"From where the swelling is and the way it's discoloring, it's obvious you've broken a bone," she mouthed off, sounding like Moses announcing the Ten Commandments. "Probably the tip of the fibula—that'll be a lateral malleolus fracture. I'll wrap it, but it really needs a cast. You'll have to keep your foot still."

"I wasn't planning on going anywhere," I growled at her. She must have missed the mean tone in my voice, or maybe she just let it fly past her, because she began to wrap my ankle with the strips of T-shirt.

After she got through playing doctor, she said, "I'm soaking wet," and started to shiver.

"Yeah, well, big surprise," I said, talking ornery because I hurt. "That's what happens when you get half drowned in a flash flood and then get dumped on by a cloudburst. I'm not so dry myself, you know. And I'm not only wet, I've got a broken foot, according to the great doctor Gina Farrell, who knows everything."

Quick as a flash, she shot back, "Everything except how to raise the IQ of that *re*ject Justin Farrell, who was stupid enough to get his foot smashed in the first place."

"Stupid!" I sputtered. "You were the stupid one! I couldn't get up out of the flood because you wouldn't move your body fast enough. Probably because you were scared to climb the Moki steps. Right? Right?" She made me so mad I banged my foot, and then I nearly sobbed because it hurt so much.

"At least you could thank me for taking care of you," Gina said, sounding so dang self-righteous I wanted to smash her.

"Thanks a lot," I snarled, "for ruining the only pair of boots I own."

"Maybe you could get them fixed."

"Yeah. Sure." That showed how much she knew about getting shoes repaired. She'd probably never had a pair fixed in her whole life. I bet if her heels wore down the least little bit, she just threw the shoes away and got herself a new pair. That must be what it's like when you don't have to worry about money.

Gina gave me a snotty look and scrambled to the back of the ledge. She sat against the curve of the overhang. There was plenty of room; we weren't crowded or anything. The ledge was about fifteen feet wide, and high enough to stand up in the middle, if I'd been able to stand.

I sat there feeling bummed out. I didn't understand why Gina and I were always at each other like wildcats in a sack. All the other girls I know seem to like me quite a lot. My three older sisters treat me as though I'm the greatest thing God put on earth since he made rainbows. Mom said that when I was a baby, she was afraid I'd never learn to walk because my big sisters always fought over which one got to carry me.

I get along okay with the girls at school, too. More than okay. A couple of times a week, girls call me up on the telephone. Sometimes it's even a toll call, if they phone all the way from Harkville. So why did Gina hate me so much?

Once in a while she'd act just great, like when she pulled me up the Moki steps. Then I'd halfway begin to like her. But before I had a chance

to like her for very long, she'd start to treat me like scum again. Gina had always been hard to get along with, but I'd never known her to be as hateful as she was that weekend. I guess she felt bad about her mother. But why did she have to take it out on me because her mother ran off to San Francisco?

A flash of lightning lit the cave; the thunder behind it was so loud it rattled my back teeth. I shot a quick look at Gina. She was huddled against the wall, her long hair all soaked and messy, the skin on her belly gone goose-bumpy where her T-shirt was too short. She had smudges under her eyes—not dirt, but tiredness. My mad shrank a little bit, because she looked worn-out and scared. I thought maybe I ought to cheer her up. Say something nice, or funny. But I couldn't think of anything either nice or funny to say, so the silence between us stretched out longer.

Just then a sheet of water began to pour off the overhang above our heads. "What's happening?" Gina gasped.

That gave me a chance to talk. "The mesa top up above us must have filled up like a saucer," I told her, almost shouting to be heard above the storm. "Now the water is spilling over the edge. It's a new-made waterfall."

"*Ooooh,*" Gina breathed, coming up closer to the edge. "I've never seen a waterfall from the back before."

Water sheeted down like a thick curtain, a pale rusty color, looking more solid than liquid. It was nearly as wide as the rock overhang above us; the curtain covered all but a small space at one edge. Through that space, you could still look out at the rain.

"There comes another waterfall," I said to Gina, pointing to the mesa rim across the gully. In a huge gush of water that made an extra roar to add to all the pounding around us, water shot off the rim to free-fall into the canyon below. Since that rim was higher than a hundred feet above the gully, its waterfall was pretty awesome.

Sometimes those waterfalls get so red and thick with mud, they seem to ooze down off the mesa tops. Ours wasn't that thick; it cascaded. "Every time there's a cloudburst around here, these waterfalls start up," I told Gina. "Then, after the rain stops, they die pretty quick."

Gina stayed quiet for a bit. In a trembly voice, she then asked, "Speaking of dying, do you suppose Jaggers is—"

"Dead? It's hard to say. He might have outrun that flood if he started soon enough, and if he

found a place to climb before the water hit. If he didn't . . . well, he's dead for sure."

"What about our fathers?" she asked, real softly.

"Oh, they'll be okay. My dad would have seen that storm coming in plenty of time to get to a safe place. I should have noticed it too, but I had other things occupying my head. Like getting shot at."

Gina stared at the sheet of water pouring in front of us, as if she wanted to memorize every thread. "It was awful, wasn't it?" she asked without looking at me. "Jaggers was trying to kill us. Now he's dead, probably. And we're alive. Probably." She smiled in a worried way, as if she wasn't sure how long we were going to stay alive.

"We'll make it," I told her. "We're tough. Besides," I joked, "you're too mean and ornery to die."

She smiled a little easier that time. Then she shivered. "I'm so wet and cold. And I must look awful," she said. "My hair is all tangled. I've got a fatal case of the frizzies."

She pulled her hairbrush out of the back pocket of her jeans and began to brush her hair. Her hand must not have been steady, either from tiredness or from cold, because she dropped the brush. It fell out of her hand, hit a rock, bounced in an arc, and shot through the curtain of water in our waterfall, to fall into the flood below.

Gina's empty hand was still up in the air, in brushing position. She looked so surprised at what had happened, and mad at herself at the same time.

"For my next trick," she said, "I will set myself on fire."

The whole thing made me laugh a great big hoot. When I could stop laughing, I said in my best hick-cowboy voice, "Waaal, ma'am, we shore could use the heat."

5.

IN THE DARK

I felt cold and miserable. Water poured down from the roof so hard that drops splashed backward into the cave. That made the cave too damp for my clothes to dry. I would have given a whole year's allowance for just one cup of hot chocolate. Well, maybe two cups. I probably would have bought one for Justin.

"How will we ever get back to . . . to my dad, and your family?" I asked him.

"Whenever the rain finally stops," Justin answered, "the flood will stop too, shortly after. Then it's up to you, Gina. You'll have to climb down the Moki steps and hike out the canyons to the highway. I feel bad the whole thing's got to be dumped on you, but . . . my foot . . ."

The trembling inside me matched my shivers

on the outside. How would I keep from getting lost in those canyons? What if I got into quicksand again? What if Jaggers *wasn't* dead? To shut out the fears, I asked, "What time is it now?"

"I don't know," Justin answered. "My watch got drowned in the flood. It's stopped running."

"Can't you tell time by the sun or something?"

"Sun!" Justin laughed at me. "If you can find me some sun behind all this rain, I'll be glad to let you know what time it is."

His laugh made me feel stupid again, as if I didn't know anything about the wilderness, which I guess I didn't, really. My dad never took me camping. Even though my dad and I both have our own horses, and I can ride nearly as well as he does, he always goes camping with his friends. How many times he's told me, "Only men are going, Gina. Some of the men are bringing their sons, but . . . no girls."

To Justin I muttered, "I was just trying to figure out how long we've been gone from our fathers. They must be worried sick about us. Do you suppose the rain will last much longer?"

"God didn't let me know what his plans are," he answered. "Maybe it will rain for forty days and forty nights."

Smart-mouth! He sounded so flip—as if he

wasn't much worried about the trouble we were in—that I just had to take a dig at him. "Justin, if I thought I'd have to spend even forty *hours* up here with you, I'd jump off this cliff right now."

I didn't expect my put-down to have such an effect on him. He started to squirm, and looked really uncomfortable.

"Hey, I didn't mean it about jumping off the cliff," I told him.

"It's not that." His face got red. Not just his ears, which always get red when he's mad, but his whole face.

"Then what?"

His face turned even redder. "I have to go to the bathroom."

I couldn't help laughing; he sounded so silly. "Well, go for it," I told him. "Don't let me stop you."

I'd forgotten he could barely move. Watching him struggle over to the ledge with his right leg dragging, I felt sorry for him. That is, until he reached the ledge and yelled at me, "For crud's sake, Gina. You could at least turn your back."

Oh, how childish and immature! "You do have hang-ups about bodies, don't you?" I called over to him.

"Maybe I do, but I think the way I feel is a lot

more normal than the way you feel. You're not even a little bit modest. Girls ought to be modest."

I snorted. Like a pig. That isn't a very polite sound to make, but Justin brings out the worst in me. "Justin," I said to him, "I'm going to be a doctor when I grow up. A surgeon, like my father. I've already studied a lot of anatomy and physiology, and I can tell you for sure—bodies are just mechanical devices. So go ahead and do what you have to do. I'm not the least bit interested, but to make it easier on your painful adolescent shyness, I'll turn around."

After a few minutes, I heard him say, "Gina, I've been thinking."

I turned to look at him. He'd made his way back to the center of the cave, and was sitting there rubbing his injured ankle.

"I've been thinking," he said again, "that you have just about the meanest, snottiest mouth I've ever heard in all my life. If I'd had to live with you, and had to listen to your mean mouth every single day, like your poor mother did, I'd have run away a lot farther than San Francisco."

You creep! I wanted to scream at him. You rotten, vicious creep! I ached to call him terrible names, but I couldn't make a sound because my throat was all choked up. When tears rushed hot

to my eyes, I squeezed back the salt. I'd never let Justin see that he'd made me cry!

Once I was in control again, I said, "Great! You'd have fallen right into the Pacific, with all the other pollution."

My voice must have sounded croaky, because Justin stared hard at me. "It's just . . . you're no older than me, but you talk so high and mighty," he said. "Like you were already a full-fledged surgeon or something. Or like God was speaking through your mouth. You really crud me out when you talk like that, Gina. I'm sorry, but you do."

Was that supposed to be an apology? Did he think I'd accept it? "You and I may be the same chronological age," I told Justin, "but mentally, emotionally, and physically, I'm superior to you. Because all girls are superior to all boys."

That made Justin turn *his* back on *me.* As he turned, he muttered a few four-letter words I managed to hear, in spite of the noise our waterfall made. Poor Justin. He couldn't even *swear* in front of a girl.

For all my brave words, I was almost sick with worry, and so cold I couldn't stop shaking. I ground my back teeth together because I didn't want Justin to hear them chatter. When at last he turned to face me again, I wasn't able to hide my shivering.

"Gina," he said, sounding way too polite, "over there by that adobe wall is an Indian pot. Would you kindly hold it under the waterfall, wash it off, fill it up, and bring it over here? I'd be glad to do it for myself if I could get around better . . . I mean, ordinarily I'd never expect a superior girl to wait on me, but—"

"Oh, shut up," I told him. Suddenly I was too cold, too exhausted, and too hurt by Justin's cruel remark about my mother to have the energy to fight with him. "Let's call a truce," I suggested tiredly.

"Fine with me. Go for the water."

The pot looked drab in the dim light of the cave, but when I lifted it to let the waterfall wash off the dust, designs leaped from its sides. Black zigzag lines painted on white glaze—beautiful! I held the pot carefully, thinking how much my mother would have admired it. Thinking how she'd have started right away to dream up a modern design based on this ancient one. Shaking my head roughly to get rid of those thoughts, I carried the pot to Justin.

"Thank you, ma'am. Set it down, please. The water's gritty—we'll have to let it settle for a while, and then it'll be fit for drinking. Wait—don't go," he said when I started to move away.

I came back again and stood over him. He looked so uncomfortable, sitting on that damp,

hard ledge. That leg should have been casted and propped up on pillows in a warm clean hospital.

"Does your leg hurt a lot?" I asked him.

"Not too much. I think this cold rock is making it numb. That's what I want to talk to you about. The cold."

He shifted around, moving his leg with his hands, rubbing his ankle. "Gina, we're going to be stuck here all night. I didn't tell you that before because I didn't want to scare you, but this storm won't let up for a long time. Maybe not till tomorrow. If we allow ourselves to get too cold right now, we'll be a lot worse off later on."

"Hypothermia," I said.

"What's that?"

"When your body temperature drops way below normal."

"I didn't know it had a name," Justin said, "but I do know we've got to save our body heat as much as we can. So . . . even though you're not too crazy about being near me, we ought to stay close together. I mean *real* close. Starting right now."

I wrinkled my nose. "I guess you're right, but . . ."

"But what!" Justin yelled. "You were the one that asked for a truce! Look, I don't feel all that great about sitting next to you either, but . . . shoot!"

"I was only going to say," I interrupted in a voice even cooler than my skin temperature, "that we'd be better off if we could fit ourselves into a smaller space. Some little corner of the cave that we could fill up. That way even less of our body heat would escape."

"Oh. Well, you're the only one of us who can walk around," he said. "So go scout out a hole for us. You better do it right now. I don't know what time it is, but seems like the light's starting to fade."

There wasn't much area for me to search. The whole ledge was no wider than my bedroom at home, and not as deep from front to back. It was scooped out of the rock, shell-shaped, like the stage in my school auditorium. That cave would have great acoustics for a band concert, I thought. It was already doing a number on the sound from the waterfall.

The only tight corner was where the stone and adobe wall joined the natural rock wall. I sat down to test it for size, gasping when the wet seat of my jeans hit the cold rock floor. If Justin and I scrunched up—pulled our knees to our chins—we could fit together in the corner and maybe keep ourselves from freezing.

Broken bits of stone and mortar littered the ground. I kicked some of them out of the way so Justin could have a clear path. "There's a place over here," I called, going back to him.

His face looked so gray when I bent to help him up; I realized that because of his injury, the trouble we were in was a lot harder on Justin than on me.

Leaning on me, with his arm across my shoulder, he hobbled to the corner I showed him. I should have held on to him longer when he bent to sit down. I let go too soon, and his bottom hit with a thud, jarring his leg, making him give an *Oof!* of pain.

"Now go bring the pot of water, so you won't have to get up again whenever we need a drink," he told me.

It felt strange to sit next to Justin and lean close to him. I mean, we'd been sniping at each other the whole weekend; our whole lives, practically. Suddenly, there we were, pressing against each other like a couple of teenagers making out at a movie theater. I guess both of us got disgusted expressions on our faces, because when we turned to look at one another, we burst out laughing.

"Well, at least one side of me is starting to warm up," Justin said.

"Yeah," I answered, "but I have two other places on me that are burning like volcanos. My heels."

He looked surprised. "Your heels?"

"Uh huh. I guess as long as I'm not going to walk around anymore, I can take off my boots now."

I bit my lower lip when I started to pull off my first boot. It was stuck to my sock, which was stuck to my flesh. Working my fingers down inside the back of my boot, I was able to separate the stiffened sock from the boot lining.

"Oh, my Lord!" Justin exclaimed when I pulled my right foot out. "Your sock's all bloody!"

"The other one too," I told him as I worked on my left boot.

"What did that?" he asked.

"My new boots. This was the first time I've ever worn them. They're not broken in."

Widening his eyes as though he couldn't believe such a thing, Justin asked, "You mean those hundred-dollar hiking boots did that to your feet?"

"Hundred-and-eighty-dollar," I corrected him. "All the time we were hiking, I wished I had your cowboy boots, because yours were all broken in."

Justin sat there shaking his head, mouth part-way open, eyes rolling as he muttered, "My twenty-nine ninety-five K-Mart blue-light spe-cials—and she wanted my boots!" Then he looked angry. "For crud's sake, Gina, why didn't you say something? If I'd known you were all bloody like that, we'd have called off the hike and gone back down the trail."

Right. Why hadn't I said something? If I had, we would never have seen the petroglyph or Jaggers. Or gotten caught in the flash flood.

The answer was simple. I'd refused to admit that I was in pain because I didn't want Justin to think I couldn't keep up with him. Simple an-swer. Stupid me.

"Here," he said, dipping his hand into the In-dian pot. "Soak the heels of your socks to dissolve the blood. Then you'll be able to get your socks off."

"Do you think I ought to take them off?" I asked. "My feet will get too cold."

"You can put the socks back on after we've washed your sores. But if you don't get that cloth pulled away from the raw places, they won't be able to scab over." He dripped water onto the bloody parts of my socks, then cupped his hands over my heels to help the water warm up and penetrate. When the socks finally came unstuck

and I pulled them off, Justin made fake gagging noises at the sight of my huge, raw blisters.

"Here I've been complaining about *my* foot," he said, "and you've been staggering around on two bloody stumps. How could you ever stand all that running down the canyon when your feet were so gory?"

"Remember what you told me before?" I reminded him. "Besides being ornery, I'm tough. Tough as iron spikes. And twice as likely to stab people with my mean mouth."

Justin nudged his shoulder against me. "Hey, Gina. I'm really sorry I took that cheap shot at you about your mother. I feel real bad that I ever said such a thing."

I pulled my knees up to my chin and hugged them. "Forget it. Maybe I deserved it. I was bad-mouthing you, too."

Our waterfall kept dumping away like Niagara Junior, but except for the noise it made, the cave was quiet. The thunder had stopped; now the rain was just a hard, steady downpour.

For a while, neither one of us had anything to say. I rested my forehead on my knees and tried to empty my mind, to push away memories of all the terrible things that had happened to us that day. After a few minutes, a weird, gurgly noise made me jerk upright, then laugh out loud. Justin's stomach had given a really huge growl. "Shut up, down there," he said, patting his stomach. "Poor old stomach, it wants fed. Feeeed me, I'm hungry! That's what it's saying."

"Mine too," I answered. "My stomach's on its knees, begging. For something hot and delicious. Let's see, what does it want? Maybe some nice scallops in herb and butter sauce, with wild rice."

"Hot dogs and beans," Justin said.

"That's too ordinary. Think of something special."

Justin licked his lips and announced, "Southern-fried chicken with mashed potatoes and giblet gravy. That puts me into hog heaven."

"I was thinking of something more gourmet, like chicken Kiev, or a lamb moussaka. Baklava for dessert."

"Well, if you're gonna go foreign—*tacos!*" he yelled. "That's Mexican."

"I know it's Mexican, you nut," I giggled. "How 'bout . . . chimichangas with chili verde?"

"How 'bout let's stop all this talk about food," Justin groaned. "It's making me drool like a hound dog."

Leaning back against the wall and closing my eyes, I said, "You know what I'd really like? A nice electric blanket."

"Yeah? Where would you put the plug?" Justin asked.

"In your mouth, stupid. Where else?"

We giggled again, but our giggles were slowing down. We'd had a wild, exhausting day. Being so close together did make us less cold and shivery, and kind of drowsy. As my eyelids started to close, and my head drooped closer and closer to Justin's shoulder, I thought of one more thing my stomach wanted. But I was so sleepy, I wasn't sure whether I said it out loud, or only said it inside my head. Warm milk. A cup of nice, warm . . .

At first my sleep was so deep that not a single dream-thought flickered through my mind. Then, slowly, I felt myself falling into fear. Jaggers was after me, chasing me through the canyon. My legs had turned to heavy stone, and it was agony to move them. Jaggers came so close behind me that his hand reached around my face. The hand was tattooed (I knew the other vandal actually had the tattoos, but in my dream it was Jaggers). He kept shooting me—*bam, bam, bam!* Instead of bullets, sword-sharp icicles came out of the gun and stabbed through me. When I turned to beg Jaggers not to kill me, I saw that his face had been tattooed with one huge skull, which melted away into a real skull, and . . .

Screams started deep inside me, in the part of me that Jaggers' icicles had speared. The screams spurted up, like vomit in my throat, until I felt arms around me, shaking me; breath against my ear from a voice shouting, "Gina, wake up! You're having a nightmare."

Was I awake or asleep? Everything looked pitch black. Too dark to tell whose arms . . . but *someone* held me tight. . . . Friend or enemy?

Then I knew I had to be awake, because the voice said, "Geez alive, you dang near scared the crap out of me with that screaming." Who but my real, live cousin Justin would say something that gross to a person coming terrified out of a nightmare!

His arms were still around me. They felt good. Maybe because I was cold, exhausted, and scared brainless from the dream; maybe because it was so dark I couldn't see Justin; maybe because we were squeezed tight into that little space—for whatever reason, I heard myself say, "This is the first real hug I've had since my mother went away."

I sucked in my breath, astonished that I'd said such a thing.

"Doesn't your father hug you?" Justin asked.

"No. He's not a huggy type of person. He kisses me on the forehead, or gives me a little pat on the back."

"My father doesn't hug me, either," Justin said. "But that doesn't bother me any, because I know he loves me. In fact, I'm glad he's not the huggy type. I get enough slobbering over from my mother and my three big sisters."

My frightening mental image of Jaggers' skull-face had almost faded away. Except for a little fluttering in my insides, I'd got over the terror enough to feel like talking. "You know, Justin, I guess that's why I've always hated you. Well, no, not really actually hated you . . . just disliked you a whole lot."

He shifted away from me a little. "Why?"

"Because your sisters and your parents always make such a huge fuss over you. Justie this, Justie that! 'Did we show you the ribbon Justie won in the barrel race?' " I mimicked. "All that hugging and attention you get, as if you're just the most maximal person in the world. Simply because you happened to be born a boy. 'At last, a son in the Farrell family, after all that trying—ha ha ha,' " I mimicked again. "As though being a boy is so much greater than being a girl."

I could feel him pull away even farther. Pretty soon he said, "Gina, if being a girl is so great, why do you want to be just like your father instead of your mother? Instead of turning into a doctor, why don't you be like your mother and make clay pots when you grow up?"

"That's the most illogical . . . That's . . . Listen, numbhead," I sputtered, "plenty of men are into ceramics, and plenty of women are into medicine. I happen to like medicine! On the nights my dad comes home for dinner, we always talk about any interesting cases he has, or the newest discoveries in medicine. I love it!"

"All right! All right! Don't get so flapped up."

"My father says I'm brilliant, that I'll make a terrific doctor."

"Well, goody for you."

Justin didn't say that in a mean way, so I calmed down. He still had his arm around me—it's hard to get mad at someone who's hugging you. I guess I'd sounded pretty witchy, so to make it up to him, I tried to think of something pleasant to talk about.

"What do you want to do when you grow up?" I asked him.

In the dark I could feel his chest fill up and then relax as he sighed. "That's a toughie. I know what I *want* to do—join the Air Force and try to make it into the space program. But my dad expects me to stay on the ranch and work it with him."

Justin wanting to be an astronaut! That's something I'd never have guessed. "You have to score really superior to get into the space program," I told him.

"I *am* superior." He didn't sound the least bit braggy, just matter of fact. "I test out at tenth-grade level in every subject. Physically, too. Let's face it, Gina, you and I are *both* superior persons."

Again my words poured out before I had any idea that I was going to let them. "If I'm so great," I choked, "why did my mother leave me?"

The tears came then, rolling down my cheeks, but silently, because I wouldn't let myself make noise crying. Justin had already seen me cry once that day, when my father fell on the rock climb. That was enough. He must have felt me stiffen, though. In a clumsy way, he pulled my head onto his shoulder and tightened his arm around me.

"Did you ever think that maybe she didn't leave *you*?" Justin asked. "Maybe she just plain left. Period." He made small motions against me, as if he were rocking a little kid. "I wonder . . . could it be that your mother got to feeling put down by all that high-powered medical talk around the supper table all the time? Maybe she just had to go someplace where people think throwing pots is important too."

That did it. The sobs wouldn't stay back for another second. I began to blubber and bawl like a baby, wailing, *"Being my mother* is important! I miss her so much! Why did she have to go away?"

"Hey, Gina!" Justin shook me. "Hey, cut it out!" Then he sort of wrapped himself around me and said, "Oh, go ahead then. Maybe you need a good cry. My sisters always say a nice, sloppy cry makes them feel better."

I had a good cry, all right. It went on and on, as though it would never stop. When I finally got so worn out I couldn't sob any more, the words started to stampede out of my mouth like *they'd* never stop, either. All about my mother. How she was always there for me. My father wasn't, because doctors have responsibilities to their patients; that's the way the medical profession has always been, the way it's supposed to be.

How Mother would come in and rub my back at night before I fell asleep, and we'd talk about everything. I guess she talked to me a lot because Dad was so often late for meals, or away at a conference, or making rounds at the hospital. On his days off, he'd want to get some fresh air —I guess he missed ranch life—so he'd go camping or climbing. With his men friends (and their sons).

That was the first time I'd even mentioned my mother in the three whole months since she'd

left for San Francisco. And to think that I spilled my guts to Justin, of all people. It might have been because we were so isolated in that cranny in the cave, in the dark, sealed off from the world by the waterfall. Like twin baby chicks inside an eggshell.

"Well, it's all over now. She's gone," I said, giving another sob that ended in a hiccup.

A long pause stretched out after that, with only the throb of the waterfall drumming against the silence. Then, "Did I ever tell you about my friend Arlen?" Justin asked.

"No, I don't think so."

Justin was silent again. From the slight tremble in his arm, I felt that whatever he was going to say was causing him some kind of hurt.

"He was my best friend," Justin finally began. "We were in the same grade—had been since kindergarten. We always sat together on the bus; one day we'd get off at my house, the next day at his. Till last year."

Another long silence. I wanted to encourage Justin to go on, so I asked, "What happened then?"

I could feel him reach down to rub his ankle, as if he still needed more time to put the words together right.

"Arlen's dad bought a motorcycle," he went on. "Not a big one, just a Yamaha 125 dirt bike.

It belonged to his dad, but Arlen was allowed to ride it. Not on the highway, because he'd have been arrested for driving without a license, but on the dirt road to their ranch. No one except Arlen could ride it—his dad made a rule about that. None of Arlen's friends. Not even me, and I was his best friend."

I waited, wondering what Justin was leading up to. I wasn't at all impatient about listening. I felt relaxed, at peace with my cousin there in the dark, willing to give him all the time he needed to say what he wanted to say.

"Well, heck fire, you can imagine how bad I wanted to ride that old Yamaha! One day, when I knew Arlen's dad had gone into Flagstaff, I begged and begged Arlen for a ride. I promised him everything I owned, just about—my transistor radio, my electronic basketball game. I even told him I'd do his homework for a month. No way! He wouldn't let me ride. I got so dang mad that I mouthed off at him, called him real scummy names. Said I was going home, and I'd never hang around with him again."

Justin gave another sigh, one that seemed to come all the way from his toes. When he spoke next, his voice was husky. "Right after I left, the Yamaha hit a chuckhole. Arlen got thrown over the handlebars. His neck broke. He died."

I could only manage to whisper, "How awful!"

"Yeah. Especially after all the cruddy things I'd said to him only a half hour before. You know, Gina," Justin's voice was muffled, "I can never take back those words, because Arlen's dead. I'll never see him again, or talk to him again."

I could tell Justin was crying, there in the dark. It was my turn to give sympathy, as much as I could drag up out of my own hurting. Feeling kind of shy about it, I reached out and put my arms around Justin. A strange, sort of satisfying, even happy feeling came over me when I did that, when I comforted him. During the past couple of months, the only warm-blooded creature I'd touched with any affection was my horse while I groomed her.

"The thing is, Gina," Justin said, thumping my knee with his fist, "your mother's alive! She's just in San Francisco. You can pick up the phone and talk to her. You can get on a bus and go visit her. Shoot, you could probably live with her if you wanted to. It *isn't* all over between the two of you."

For the first time in my life, I think I felt real love for my cousin. "Oh, Justie, do you suppose she'd really want to see me?"

"Sure," he answered. "Aren't you a maximal person?"

6.

OVER THE CHASM

It was so ding-blasted cold that neither of us got much sleep during the night, but I guess we dozed off now and again. Gina had nightmares all night long. I could tell by the way she moaned and twitched. She cried out in her sleep, sometimes for her mother, sometimes for her dad.

My own dreams weren't all that great, either. Over and over again I saw the BLM archaeologist falling, his mouth making a silent round O as he got sucked down into empty space.

About the hundredth time I woke up, I could just barely make out the outline of Gina's head, so I knew the sky was starting to turn into morning. Somehow, even that tiny little hint of light made me feel better. Nothing is worse than absolute pitch-black darkness in a strange, empty place.

Feeling more relaxed, I slept deeper. Probably because it got a little warmer too. In one of my groggy, half-awake flashes, I noticed the rain had stopped. Our waterfall was no longer a solid wet curtain; it was now just a bunch of individual drops falling from the ledge overhang.

"That's good," I thought, rolling over and going back to sleep. Both Gina and I were stretched out on the rock by that time. Gina was sleeping hard, I guess because of all the crying and truth-spilling she'd done during the night. Letting go your emotions like that can leave you zonked out afterward, I know.

Later on, still more asleep than awake, I batted my hand around my ear to chase away a wasp. The wasp's buzzing didn't go away. When the sound finally pushed through my sleep, I leaped up so fast that the pain in my leg nearly knocked me down again. That noise was no wasp! It was an airplane!

"Gina!" I yelled, lunging for her and shaking her hard. "Wake up! There's a plane up there." From the motor, I figured it was a small, single-engine outfit.

"Mmmm, what?" Gina mumbled, still in the zonk zone.

"Get up! Get up!" I was almost screaming in my excitement. "That plane might be searching for us. We've got to signal it."

She scrambled to her feet, not altogether alert but at least moving. "Signal! How?"

"I don't know how! Think!" I was really screaming by that time, because the motor noise seemed slightly farther away.

That Gina, she has the fastest problem-solving reflexes of anyone I know. She ran to the rim of the ledge and peered up at the sky. "I see it," she shouted. "There it is. And the sun's shining. We can signal the plane with my mirror."

Wow! Great thinking! "Where is your mirror?" I yelled.

She slapped her jeans pockets, then frantically dug her hands into one pocket after another. "I can't find it. Help me, Justie!"

My leg hurt so bad you wouldn't believe it, but I scrambled around on two hands and one knee like a hyper turtle, looking for the broken pieces of Gina's pocket mirror.

"Here it is!" I yelled in triumph, holding up the biggest piece of mirror. It had been half buried in the dirt.

"Thank God!" Gina said. "The plane's circling now. If we don't do something fast, it will fly away." Then she turned to me with the most terrible, helpless look. "Oh, Justie, how will I manage to signal it? The sun's all the way over there, across the gully."

Our ledge was situated about a quarter of the

way up, in a mesa that stood on the east side of the canyon. Since it was still early in the morning, the sun hung in the east, *behind* us. It was shining like crazy on the mesa across the canyon from us, but our mesa was in shadow. How could we catch sun on a mirror when we were all covered with shade?

"Maybe you could climb down the Moki steps real fast . . ." I started to suggest. "No, that wouldn't work either."

The two high rock walls were close enough together that our mesa shaded the bottom part of the wall opposite us. Even if Gina did get down the Moki steps in time, she'd have had to climb partway up the opposite wall to reach the sun. And there was no way for her to climb it. No Moki steps over there.

"Justin, come here. Fast!" Gina motioned me toward the rim of the ledge. "You'll have to hold me. If I can lean out far enough, I might be able to reach the sunlight with the mirror."

Somehow I got over to the edge, where I could see a patch of blue sky overhead, and a small plane that looked about the size of a dragonfly. It circled slowly in the clear, cloudless air. Every trace of storm was gone. Beneath us, the flood was gone too, although it had left a lot of muck behind.

I noticed all that in a microsecond. Then I had

to use all my smarts to figure out a way to hold Gina, since I was not at my physical best because of a bum leg. I could picture exactly what it was she wanted to do.

"Over here," I told her, pointing to the narrow left corner of the ledge, where the ceiling sloped down to meet the floor. Right at that point, a boulder of reddish sandstone had gotten stuck in the jaws of the ledge. It was too big to have fallen down with all its smaller boulder buddies when the earth shook them loose, about a million years before, at the time the cave first fissured open.

I wrapped my good left leg around the base of the boulder, and my left arm around the top of it. I knew I'd be safe—that heavy old rock wasn't about to move anywhere.

I'd be safe, but what Gina was planning scared me so much that my arm hairs stood straight up. Funny, we'd hardly said any words about it, but my mind knew exactly what it was she had in her mind. She wanted me to brace her while she hung way out over empty space. With her body stretched out holding that little piece of mirror, she hoped to catch a piece of sunbeam to signal the plane.

"Maybe it's too dangerous. You better not try it . . ."

"Shut up," she said. "Hold my hand tight and

don't let go. Oh, Lord help me, I'm so scared!"

Gina weighs about the same as I do, maybe a few pounds more. Straining with every bit of strength in me, I squeezed that boulder with my left arm and leg. My right arm was pulled out like a gum band, my hand clutching Gina's hand.

She'd got both her feet—wearing those thick, useless socks, because she didn't have time to put her boots on—braced right along the edge of the rim. Pulling on me so tight I thought she'd yank my shoulder out of the socket, Gina leaned out over empty nothing and held the mirror toward the sun.

Those rays of sunlight were only inches beyond her reach, so close that we could see a little fluffy bird feather fluttering around—a tiny bit of sunlit fuzz—in the updraft from the canyon. Gina and I stretched, groaning, toward the shaft of sunlight.

Two thousand feet above the bird feather, the single-engine plane, painted silver with red stripes on the wings, droned sweet as a honeybee while it floated away from us.

"Farther. Lean me out farther," Gina said through tight teeth. My own teeth were gritted just as tight, and I was fighting hard to keep from clamping my eyes shut, because oh, Lord, was I scared too, holding on to my cousin as she

stretched over a deep chasm and if my hand got sweaty or her hand slipped, it was a long way down and she'd get . . . The dream wasn't yet gone that far out of my mind, about the BLM man plunging down, with his lips shaped into an O. . . .

And then . . . Gina dropped the mirror.

"No, no, no, NO!" she screamed, as I pulled her quickly back. "Oh, why am I so stupid! Why can't I ever do anything right?" She fell onto my chest and started to sob again. I do guarantee, between the rainstorm and the flash flood and all the tears Gina cried against me, that was the wettest weekend I ever spent.

"I'm just a failure!" she wailed.

"Oh, bulldunkie! Is it your fault the sun's where it is?" I asked her. "Or that our arms are too short?"

She cried a little more, then quietened down. In the silence, I could just barely make out the airplane's motor, moving away from us, now no louder than a whisper.

"Well," Gina said, smearing her teary cheeks with the backs of her hands, "what do we do now?"

I hated to tell her what she had to do, because she already looked so bummed out. The dark smudges underneath her eyes had turned into puffy dark circles. Her long hair had gotten tangled into an awful mess. Her torn T-shirt was all slopped with dirt, and the heels of her socks looked stiff from dried, darkened blood.

"Never mind. You don't have to tell me," she said, saving me from the need to say it. "I have to hike out and find help, right?"

"Yes ma'am. I'm afraid that's right."

Looking worn out but brave (so brave it made my insides give a twist of . . . respect, or something) she picked up her boots to put them on.

"Wait. Give your feet a little more time to rest," I told her. "First I'll try to show you which way you have to go."

I moved to a part of the ledge we hadn't yet walked or sat on, where the dust was still smooth and unmarked. With my finger, I began to draw a map in the dirt.

"As long as you start out in the right direction from here," I said, "—and that's no problem, because I'll be watching to see that you do—you can't get lost coming out of this particular canyon."

In a low, worried voice, she asked, "What about the quicksand?"

"Try to picture where it was. Remember the ledge I was on, and the big pile of boulders you jumped off." Even while I said that, I knew that

the canyon was going to look quite different, today, from what it had been yesterday. Because of the flood. That big pile of boulders might have gotten knocked right apart, or it could have instead been built up to twice as high, from branches and rocks washing down on it and getting stuck. And Lord!—oh, Lord! What if Jaggers' body had gotten stuck on it too?

"Try to stay up above the canyon floor," I told her. "The bottom will be full of muck, anyway. Wherever there's a ledge you can climb up onto, walk on it. Only whatever you do, don't get yourself rimrocked."

"Rimrocked?"

"That's when you keep climbing from one ledge or boulder to another, higher and higher. Then, all of a sudden, you can't figure out how you got to where you are. Can't see a way to get up any higher, or any way to get down. That's rimrocked."

Gina's eyes got real big. What a terrible, awful thing I was doing, sending my poor cousin for help, when she didn't know a dang thing about that rugged, wild country. Since I'd scared her so much, talking about getting rimrocked, I had to think of a way to calm her down.

"When you get to the end of this side canyon, you'll for sure be able to recognize the trail we came down yesterday. No problem at all," I told her. Yeah, no problem. Would she recognize anything, after the mess the flash flood made? "You don't want to make a left turn there, which is the way we would have gone back to where our fathers were climbing," I said. "Instead, take a right."

"A right," she repeated, her forehead all scrunched in a frown, like she was trying so hard to remember everything I said. "Make a right turn at the bottom of the trail."

"That'll take you down a much wider canyon. After about a mile, you come to a jeep trail." How would she know it was a jeep trail, if the tire tracks were all washed away?

"Turn left there. Hike two more miles," I said, "and you'll hit the highway. Enough cars come by that way that someone will pick you up."

Poor old Gina. She looked a little sick. I couldn't blame her. I was scared spitless myself, sending her out alone into that empty, dangerous land.

"Look," I said, "you might not have to go anywhere near that far before someone finds you. They've got to be out looking for us, you know."

"Sure," she said, like she didn't believe it. When she shoved a foot into her boot, her pale face got even paler, showing a white ring of pain

around her mouth. I got a lump inside, realizing she'd have to hike on those poor, sore heels.

"Wait, take your boot off again," I said. "Let me give you my socks. At least that way you won't have caked blood rubbing against your sores."

"That might be better," she agreed.

Gina had wrapped those strips of torn T-shirt right over the sock on my foot, so we had to undo the bandages to get my sock off. Good thing it was a tube sock that stretched, or it would have hurt too much to take off.

When I got a look at my bare ankle, sweat broke out on my face. The swelling was colored the grungiest purple-black-yucky green color anyone ever did see. If I'd had anything in my stomach, I'd have gagged it right up.

"I'd better wrap it again," Gina said. As she wound the strips of cloth around my ankle, I realized that she really was good at that kind of stuff. Once I took a first-aid course in 4-H, but I could never manage to get an ankle bandage to come out like Gina's did.

Finally there wasn't any more reason to wait. "Well," she said, trying to sound like her usual flip self, "here goes Gina into hell. Pray for her, saints."

Once again I felt a tug inside me, caused by

her courage. Way to be, Gina, I said, only I didn't say it out loud.

Flattening myself on my belly with my head over the rim of the ledge, I watched her climb down the Moki steps. She went down slowly, which gave me a chance to get a good look at the canyon.

The ground was wet, but not sloppy wet at that particular place, because it was so pebbly that the water had sunk in. The canyon walls had a high-water mark that showed how far up the flood had reached. Awesome! Must have been twelve feet above ground, near as I could tell from looking down on it. Bits of debris were stuck on the wall at the high-water mark.

Other debris lay scattered all over the place. Soggy, uprooted sagebrush and rabbitbrush, branches split off from spruce trees—they'd had to be washed down from far away, because there are no spruce trees for miles around that spot. Pieces of garbage from campgrounds located Lord knows where. Pine cones, leaves, sticks. A fresh gouge in the rock wall across from us showed where a big boulder had smacked into it with the speed of a racing car.

And there went old Gina, down those Moki steps into that desolation. I could see the top of her head, getting lower and lower.

When she reached bottom, she turned her face up to me.

"That way!" I yelled, pointing the direction she should take.

"Okay," she hollered back. "Wish me luck!"

"I do." Man, did I ever wish her luck! How I wished it was me going, instead of her.

I watched till she went out of sight around a bend. At the last minute, she turned and waved to me. I could see how stiff she'd been walking, like her heels hurt something awful but she didn't want to let on. All those miles she had to go! If I kept on worrying my head over it, I'd likely go crazy, so I stretched out on the ledge and tried to put Gina out of my mind.

Daylight had gotten pretty bright by then, though the sun wasn't yet shining into the ledge. Lying on my back, I looked up at the ceiling and got a sudden . . . "thrill" might be a dumb word for a guy to use, but that's what I got. A thrill. Because there on the ceiling was some Indian art, which I hadn't noticed in the dimness of the day before.

It was a pictograph, a painted picture. Not a picture chipped into the rock—that's a petroglyph. And guess who the pictograph on the ceiling was of? My old friend, the flute player.

Of course he looked a little different—it was a

different kind of rock art, done by a different artist, maybe in a different century—but I felt as if a kind-hearted, caring relative had come to tell me not to worry, that everything was going to turn out okay.

I lay there, relaxed, with my bad leg stretched out and my good leg bent at the knee, having a sort of wordless talk with the flute player. Sunlight slid in over the rim of the ledge, slowly reaching me. It felt great, because my clothes were still damp. I've heard of people who don't have anything to do but watch the grass grow. I had nothing to do but watch the steam rise out of my clothes. The sun was baking them dry. That, and talk to the flute player, and sleep.

His flute song twisted through my dreams. Once I woke up, sweaty, because the sunlight had turned hot. When I moved to the cooler part of the ledge, behind the stone-and-adobe storage wall, that made me think about Gina. How we'd sat there the night before. So then I couldn't go back to sleep.

I started to chew my fingernails, not just because I was worried, but because I was so starved it felt good to have *anything* inside my mouth. A little water still stood in the Indian jar, but if I had to spend another night on the ledge, my body would start to dry out. I crawled to the rim

and squinted down, straining to see motion, any sign of life in the direction Gina had gone. Nothing moved, except a shimmer of mist from the sun drying up the dampness.

Feeling chilled inside from fear, in spite of the heat on my outsides, I rolled over and put an arm across my eyes. I don't know how long I stayed like that. A long time. The sun was starting to reach down toward the top of the mesa across from me. That was west.

Suddenly I heard voices, not too loud at first, but then came a voice loud and clear calling, "Justin!"

I dove for that rim so fast it's a pure wonder I didn't go over it head first. The canyon was still empty—altogether empty. No one there. How could it be empty, when I'd heard that call so clear? Maybe I was getting spacey.

There it came again. "Justin. Up here!"

I twisted around to look up. A hundred feet above my head, Gina, my dad, and Uncle Dylan waved down at me. They'd come in over the top of the mesa!

I yelled a lot of things about how glad I was to see them, and that I was okay, and they yelled back that they'd get me out of there sooner than you could spit in a can.

Lying on my back, with my head stuck out of

the cave like a worm sticking out of an apple, I watched my dad and Uncle Dylan get ready to rescue me.

I could see them put four wedges, called 'nuts,' into cracks near the mesa rim. That, I knew, was to make a good anchor for the rope, with backups for safety, in case one of the nuts failed. After that they attached a rope and let it drop down to me.

"Bullseye!" I yelled. The rope hung right across the opening of my ledge, with the end dangling about twenty feet beneath me. I reached out to give them the thumbs-up sign, realizing as I looked up that it was quite some distance they were going to have to drag me up.

I waited, wondering who was going to come down to get me. My father, or Uncle Dylan? It turned out to be Uncle Dylan. He rappelled down that rope so fast that instinct made me yank my head back into the cave. Not that he'd land on me or anything—Uncle Dylan was too skilled a climber for that.

Uncle Dylan sure doesn't waste time. The second his feet touched the rim, he jumped inside and started to unhook the carabiner clips from his harness. Before I knew it, he had his backpack off and open, and was kneeling beside me.

"Here," he said, handing me a plastic bag full

of trail mix. "You must be starved. Gina was. Here's a bottle of water too. While you're eating, I'll take a look at that ankle."

If I thought Gina was good at bandaging ankles, her touch could be called hammer-handed compared to Uncle Dylan's. His fingers knew just what to do, where to probe, and he didn't even hurt me, not hardly at all.

"What an instinct that Gina has!" Uncle Dylan boasted, grinning at me. "She said it was probably a lateral malleolus fracture, a break at the bottom tip of the fibula. I'll lay you twenty-to-one odds that's what the X rays will show. She's going to make some great surgeon!"

His pride in her was so easy to see, it made me wonder why Gina didn't realize how he felt about her. Because I'd picked up on that, all right—that Gina didn't think her father, or anyone, loved her very much.

Even though my mouth was full of raisins and nuts and granola from the trail mix, I started to ask questions. I had so many to ask! "Is Gina okay? Where did she find you?"

"She's worn out, but she'll be fine," Uncle Dylan answered as he took an Ace bandage from his pack. "*We* found *her*. When you kids didn't come back yesterday, Bill notified the jeep posse. They started a search first thing this morning. But Bill and I had already decided to make our own search on horseback."

He told me they'd taken the first-aid kit and as much climbing gear as they could stuff into two backpacks, figuring they might need all that when they found us. The jeep posse had loaned them a radio handset so everyone could keep in radio contact. On horseback, my dad and Uncle Dylan could travel into much narrower canyons than the jeeps would be able to fit through.

"First we rode up the trail to the petroglyph," he said. "We found your hat there, Justin, so we radioed the jeep posse that you'd evidently gone that way. After we searched the whole mesa top and didn't find you, we rode back down. Right at the bottom of the trail we saw Gina coming toward us."

I guess Uncle Dylan isn't the type of person to show his fears too much. As he was telling me those things, he'd been wrapping my ankle with some thick surgical dressing pads and the Ace bandage. His hands were as steady as granite while he talked. When he got to the place where he told about finding Gina, though, I noticed his eyelids twitch.

"What about the BLM archaeologist?" I asked.

"They've found him. Right after we caught sight of Gina, we got a radio message that the

posse was sending in a helicopter to pick up the BLM man."

"His body, you mean."

"No. The BLM man himself. He's alive."

"Alive!" I couldn't believe it. "How could he fall into that deep chasm and still be alive?"

"He didn't fall all the way down. They found him on a ledge no more than forty feet below the petroglyph. He's in bad shape—multiple fractures and bleeding—but at least they say he's still alive."

What a relief that was, to learn that the man had a chance to make it. But there were still two more people I had to ask about. "Jaggers? And the other vandal?"

"No sign of those two yet." Uncle Dylan finished wrapping my foot and began to repack the first-aid kit. I needed to talk fast if I wanted more questions answered.

"How did you know where to find me?" I asked.

He zipped up the pocket he'd put the first-aid kit into. "From where we found Gina, we figured this had to be the canyon you were in. Your dad knew a way to ride in over the mesa top. We didn't want to bring the horses through the gully because of the quicksand."

"Could you see this ledge from up above?"

"No, but it wasn't hard to deduce where you were. With binoculars we could see where Gina's footprints started in the mud directly beneath you," he told me, as he began to pull pieces of climbing gear out of the backpack.

Funny, he looked so much like my father, kneeling there. Sounded like him, too, though Uncle Dylan often uses bigger words. Yet no one would ever have any trouble telling the two of them apart.

Even though they were born on the same day, my dad looks older. His face is browner and has more and deeper lines, especially around the eyes. That's from working out in the open, in the bright sun, all the time.

Their two pairs of hands show the most difference. They're the same size and shape, but Uncle Dylan's hands are always clean and smooth. His are surgeon's hands, and he takes good care of them—he wore leather gloves when he rappelled down the rope.

My dad's hands are rough, calloused, and cracked. The hands of a hard-working rancher.

Deep inside, Dylan's eyes look sad, as though he's spent too much time in a world of hurt. Once I heard him telling my dad that surgeons can make themselves feel detached, even when they're operating on their multi-hundredth motorcycle-crash victim, but they never get desensitized to the suffering they see.

The kind of doctoring my father gets to do—delivering brand-new foals and baby calves—gives a person a good feeling, makes him feel lit-up inside. My father has happy eyes. I decided that between Bill and Dylan, I was glad I'd gotten Bill for a father. Rough hands, wrinkled face, mortgaged ranch, and everything.

"Do you know how to put on a harness?" Uncle Dylan asked, but before I could answer, he said, "I'll help you."

He fitted a sling harness made of nylon webbing around my hips like you'd diaper a baby.

"Now, this isn't going to be too tricky or dangerous or anything like that," Uncle Dylan said, "but you've got to be alert and pay attention to what I tell you." As he talked, he attached a loop of webbing to the harness hook. Then he clipped a carabiner through another loop of webbing and attached it to a jumar, a kind of clamp.

"Don't worry about that fracture of yours," he went on. "It's not too serious, and I've got it well padded so it won't hurt you on your way up. When we get you to the hospital in Flagstaff, I'll cast it myself."

Holding two clamps out in front of me, he said, "You'll have two of these jumars, one for each hand. They clip onto the rope. You'll slide them up the rope, one jumar after the other. One will hold up your seat harness, the other will hold your uninjured foot in a loop. That way you can pull yourself right up the rock face."

"What! Me? Pull myself?" My voice cracked. "I thought my dad was going to pull me up, from above." I'd never climbed a sheer rock face before, even when I *didn't* have a fractured fibula.

"This will be the safest way," Uncle Dylan said. "Nothing to worry about. Just remember to keep your injured leg away from the rock so it won't get bumped."

I don't know whether I was more scared or more excited. Both, I guess, about equal. With my uncle supporting me, I hopped to the rim of the ledge. I looked up, then down. Both directions made cold things squish around in my stomach.

Uncle Dylan clipped the jumars to the rope. Then he eased me back, so that I was in a sitting position, dangling over space, supported by the seat harness.

"All right, now," he said, "put your good foot into that loop of webbing on the other line, but don't bear down on the loop. Just let your foot relax." I did what he told me. "Now slide the jumar on that loop line as high up the rope as it will reach."

I did that.

"Okay. Now stand straight up on your good foot."

When I stood up straight, the length of webbing attached to my harness went slack. "Next, move the harness-line jumar as high as it will go," Dylan told me.

I was beginning to get the picture: Sit, raise the foot loop. Stand, raise the seat harness.

It was easy! It was fun! I was moving right up that old rope like a little monkey toy I used to have when I was a kid.

From the ledge beneath me, Uncle Dylan called up instructions, telling me I was doing real good. "Stop and rest whenever you feel tired," he called. "Those lines will support you." Another time, when I got too close to the rock wall and scraped myself, he yelled, "Push away with your left arm."

Before that, I'd never climbed anything except beginners' cliffs. I'd never used any equipment that fancy, never sat in a harness over empty space. It was great, a real kick. I wasn't tired or anything, but once, for a couple of minutes, I just stopped and hung there.

Dangling over that chasm, I thought that might be what it's like to be an astronaut, suspended in space. Exploring new worlds.

I had a face-to-face look at that red sandstone

wall like no one had ever seen before. Except Uncle Dylan, and he'd rappelled down it too fast to notice the scenery.

The sun was setting behind me, deepening the colors in the rock. Just inches in front of my eyes, I could see each little knob on the rock, each tiny fissure, each grain of sandstone the color of rust or mustard or blood. No wonder Indians called canyonlands the land of the sleeping rainbow.

From above me, my father called down, "Are you all right, Justie?"

Even from that distance, I could see how worried he looked. "Fine, Dad," I answered. "I'm just fine." Better quit fooling around (hanging around?), I thought, and start up again. Pull up the foot loop, pull up the seat harness; sit, stand, sit, stand. I was moving up about six to twelve inches at a time.

As I neared the top of the mesa, my father reached down and lifted me over the edge. "Thank God, thank God," he said. For once, he squeezed me tight in a bear hug.

That hundred feet of distance had taken me more than half an hour to climb. After I reached the top, Uncle Dylan zapped up the same distance in seven minutes.

7.

BEYOND DANGER

My mother stopped the car in front of the United States Department of the Interior office in Flagstaff. As she leaned across me to open the door she asked, "Do you think this will take very long?"

"I don't know," I answered. "We have to tell them about everything that happened at the petroglyph. It's for their report, so they can prosecute Volkins."

Volkins, we'd learned, was the name of the vandal with the tattoo. He'd been caught. The other man, Jaggers, they found washed up three and a half miles farther down the canyon. He'd drowned in the flash flood.

"Well, I hope these people don't keep you too long," Mother said. "At least you got a good sleep

last night at Uncle Bill's. You look a lot better today, Gina."

"So do you, Mom."

My poor mother. The minute my father phoned her in San Francisco to tell her that Justin and I were missing, she'd jumped into her car and driven straight through to Arizona. Seventeen hours on the road, driving all alone, stopping only to buy gas. No wonder her eyes looked red and gritty.

"I'll come back here for you in about an hour," she told me. "Your dad and I are going to lunch now."

I guess I must have looked hopeful, because she said in a gentle voice, "Don't get any wrong ideas in your head, sweetheart. There's no chance that Dad and I will get back together. But we've got to talk about you, figure out how we're going to share you."

Funny. I'd thought neither of them wanted me very much. And here all those months, it turned out, they'd been fighting over who got to keep me. I'd just learned about it that morning.

Mother watched me as I walked up the sidewalk to the government agency, almost as if she were afraid someone might snatch me away. At the door I turned and waved to her, but she waited until I got inside the building before she drove off.

Inside, Justin stood in the lobby, leaning on two aluminum crutches that were shaped funny, like crooked shepherds' staffs with handles. The right leg of his jeans was split to the knee, to allow room for a plaster cast that reached from just below his knee to his toes.

"Where is everyone?" I asked, looking around.

"My mom and dad have gone to buy a load of groceries," he answered. "Food's cheaper here, in the Flagstaff supermarkets, than it is in Harkville."

"Where are all the government people?"

"They're off. It's Labor Day. No one's here but the district administrator—the guy we're supposed to talk to—but he had to go inside his office to make some phone calls." Justin shifted on his crutches. "Notice anything in this room?"

A couple of desks, maps on the walls . . . and then I saw what he meant. "The petroglyph!" I exclaimed, going up close to where it was leaning against a wall. "At last I get to see it up close." I'd never had the chance, on the day we climbed the trail.

The petroglyph looked exactly the way Justin had described it. A flute player, showing red where his outline had been chipped through the darker desert varnish, faced a bighorn sheep. They could have been carved just the day before, they were so perfect.

"Some rangers brought it down from the mountain," Justin told me. "Lucky—when Volkins let go, the rock slabbed off just the right way. Didn't get a single crack in it."

I asked, "What are they going to do with it?"

"Give it to a museum someplace. They don't know which one yet."

Tracing my finger along the outline of the sheep, I wondered how Justin felt about the petroglyph going to a museum. He'd considered it his own private property. "That won't be so bad, will it?" I asked him. "I mean, that way lots of people will get to see it and appreciate it."

"I don't mind," he said, with a sort of I've-got-a-secret smile. "The next time you come here for a visit, I'll show you why I don't feel all that bad about the petroglyph going away."

Since Justin and I had only begun to feel close to each other such a little while before, I hated to tell him my news. "I doubt that I'll get back to visit you again, Justie. From now on, it looks as if I'll be spending all my vacations in San Francisco with my mother."

"Oh."

I've heard of faces falling; that's exactly what Justin's did.

"That's too bad," he said. "I mean, it's good that you'll get to be with your mother, but I'm sorry you won't get to see the special . . . oh, shoot!"

He seemed so disappointed that I was surprised. "We could write," I suggested, "and exchange ribbons. I'll send you the ribbons I win at track meets, and you send me the ribbons you win barrel racing."

"Yeah. Even if my horse isn't a purebred like yours, he's sure good at barrel racing. Wish you'd have a chance to watch me race him some day."

Justin sounded so gloomy when he said that, he made me feel gloomy too. Then I had a wonderful idea. "Why don't you come to San Francisco to visit Mother and me?"

"Can't afford to."

"My father could pay. . . ."

"No."

That Justin, he's so much like my father. Won't accept anything from anyone, has to do everything for himself. My father left the ranch at seventeen and worked his way all through the university and medical school, earning every single penny it took. All by himself.

And Uncle Bill's the same way. He won't take a cent from my father to help with the mortgage on the ranch.

Uncle Bill and my father. Justin . . . and I. The four of us have so many traits in common.

"You know what?" I said to Justin. "This morning my father told me that, biologically, you and I are half-brother and half-sister. It's as though we had different mothers but the same father, since our fathers are genetically identical, being twins. I guess that's why you and I are so much alike."

"Alike!" he yelped. "You and me? I can't think of any two people who are *less* . . . !" He sputtered to a stop, then got a strange, thoughtful look on his face. "Could be some truth to that," he said slowly. "I guess, when you take time to think about it, you and I really are alike, in some ways. It's kind of amazing."

While he was still mulling over that amazing idea, I told him, "Being your first cousin was okay, I guess. Not great, but okay. But as for being your half-sister, genetically speaking . . . well, I think that's just—*maximal!*"

A quick flush climbed up Justin's neck and reddened his cheeks.

"And you know what else?" I went on, my voice galloping into the squeaky upper range. "I'll bet if I told my mother how much it means to me to come here, she'd let me spend at least one week each summer with you."

At first Justin didn't answer. He just flashed me a smile so huge it nearly sliced his face in half. I got the impression he really wanted me to come.

Justin could never say that, of course. So he drawled, "My heck, ma'am. If that don't sound like purty talk you jest spoke. Them nice words cain't be comin' out of that mean old buzzard-tongued Gina I've always knowed."

Grabbing one of Justin's aluminum crutches, I said, "Pardner, I'm gonna get you for that." I took a swing at him with the crutch.

"Hey! Not fair!" he yelled. "My leg's in a cast."

"So? I'll stand on one foot."

By the time the government official came into the lobby, Justin and I were laughing so hard we could hardly stay up. It's a good thing we had to stop our fake swordfight right then, because neither of us ever would have won it.

We're just too evenly matched.

Checked by experts in the United States natural resource agencies, the Mountain West Adventures are being written by GLORIA SKURZYN-SKI, author of *What Happened in Hamelin*, a Christopher Award winner. This author's ability to research and explain medicine, geography, and specific phenomena is equalled by her flair for characterization and suspense.

Gloria Skurzynski lives in Salt Lake City, Utah.